# By These Ten Bones

CLARE B. DUNKLE

# By These Ten Bones

Henry Holt and Company

New York

Henry Holt and Company, LLC
*Publishers since 1866*
115 West 18th Street
New York, New York 10011
www.henryholt.com

Library of Congress Cataloging-in-Publication Data
Dunkle, Clare B.
By these ten bones / Clare B. Dunkle.—1st ed.
p.    cm.
Summary: After a mysterious young wood carver with a
horrifying secret arrives in her small Scottish town, Maddie gains his
trust—and his heart—and seeks a way to save both him and her
townspeople from an ancient evil.
ISBN-13: 978-0-8050-7496-3
ISBN-10: 0-8050-7496-1
[1. Werewolves—Fiction.   2. Wood carvers—Fiction.   3. Secrets—
Fiction.   4. Courage—Fiction.   5. Scotland—Fiction.]   I. Title.
PZ7.D92115By 2005
[Fic]—dc22            2004052359

First Edition—2005
Book designed by Amy Manzo Toth
Printed in the United States of America on acid-free paper. ∞

1  3  5  7  9  10  8  6  4  2

*For my parents, Bill and Mary Buckalew,*
*who taught me by their example that*
*in the battle of good and evil,*
*each of us can make a difference.*

# By These Ten Bones

# prologue

"Best if you was dead."

The two of them sat at a small fire far away from dwellings, and the night wind was cold. Trees creaked and rustled in the darkness, unseen and alarming. The man was old, with tough skin and greasy gray hair. He wiped his streaming eyes on his sleeve and threw a stick into the fire with savage ferocity, sending up a shower of sparks. "Best if you was dead and with your folks," he sobbed. "You'd beg me if you knew."

The little boy stared into the flames, his face white and pinched. He didn't know what he was doing there. He didn't know who the man was. His life had become a terrifying riddle, and he was too young to make sense of it all.

"It's the only kind thing," insisted the man brokenly. "But I ain't got the guts. You'd kill me. I don't know how, but you'd do it. You're hell spawn now, that's what you be. I got to keep you alive."

The child huddled in a tunic that was much too big for him. Faint stains marked his arms and hands. They hadn't cleaned it all off. Black lines under his fingernails. Blood looked black at night. He raised frightened green eyes to the man.

"Nay, don't look on me!" was the frenzied response. "I can't bear it, I tell you! You're cursed now, understand me? Don't look on no one again. Don't be getting fond of me because I keeps you, neither. You're the kind that kills them they love."

The wind rose, flattening the lonely little fire and whipping the invisible branches of the trees. Wet leaves stirred and flopped on the ground, too heavy to fly away. The boy wrapped his thin arms around himself and tried to understand. *How could I kill anyone?* he wanted to ask. *I didn't kill them. I saw what did.* But he wasn't supposed to speak.

"Don't tell me about 'em. Not a word. I don't want to know. I can't change nothing. I can't help 'em now. Don't cry for 'em, neither, hear me? Don't go whimpering after your dam." The man collapsed, weeping noisily onto his soiled and bloody fists.

But the little boy didn't cry for his mother. He didn't shed a tear. He was in such pain of so many different kinds that he felt only bewildered surprise. He held his grandfather's wood-carving tools in their beautiful leather holder, clutching the solid form close against the torment that he felt. Only one thing was clear to him in the whirling chaos of his life. Yesterday they had belonged to his father. Today they were his.

1

In the far northern hills of Scotland, a gray castle
stood by a narrow lake, or a loch, as it is properly
called. Some castles are grand and beautiful, but this
one was not. It was too small to be grand, for one
thing, being the simplest type of castle. It had no
moat, although its builders knew it had a natural
defense: the waters of the loch at its back and
swampy ground to the front. It had no palisade
enclosing a fortified courtyard or lofty battlements.
It was merely a large, rectangular stone building
three floors high, with narrow windows through
which an archer could safely shoot his foes. Carved
into the rock floor of the lowest level was a primitive

dungeon cell, no more than a hole, and resting above the highest level was a wooden roof that no longer kept out all the rain. A round tower clung to one corner, housing a rough spiral stair.

The wide doorway that opened into this tower lacked a door. No guards stood there, and no watch-dogs barked. A clan chief had once lived here with his family and warriors, but he had lost this valley in battle long years before. A strange old woman occu-pied his castle now, to the disgust of those few of his distant kin who still farmed the fields nearby.

A girl just old enough to be thought a young woman stood inside the tower doorway and wished that the castle still had a door to close. She was dressed in the plainest of blouses, a drab skirt that tied with a lace, and a voluminous woolen wrap that looked like a long, narrow blanket. This blanket, looped around the waist and pulled over one shoul-der, was the most important clothing of the day. Hers was checked and crossed by lines and squares of yellow, gray, and brown. If it was somewhat bet-ter made than the blankets her neighbors wore, this showed only that the local weaver had his prefer-ences. Maddie could be considered a strong favorite of his: she was his only child.

Maddie herself was not particularly striking, neither tall nor short, thin nor heavy. Her straight brown hair and brown eyes did not attract attention, and if her round face was not ugly, it also was not beautiful. At least, it was not beautiful at the moment. When she smiled or laughed, her whole appearance changed. But Maddie wasn't smiling now. She was anxious and afraid.

She had almost stepped out of the shelter of the castle tower before she saw the strangers. Four men she didn't know were walking along the gravel shore of the loch, leading two pack ponies. The first two men were small and dark, dressed as her own men dressed, wearing knee-length shirts, wrapped in blankets checked white and black, their legs bare down to their sandals. The last two men were for-eigners in tunics, breeches, and boots. One of them was old, and the other was young.

Maddie shrank back into the gloom of the tower. She saw strangers very rarely. Once or twice a year, summer Travelers came through, selling or trading their craft goods. These men might be Trav-elers, or they might be wandering bandits, and their arrival frightened the girl. Four men were enough to do great harm in a settlement as small as hers.

The newcomers paused on the path by the grim old castle, but they didn't come toward it. The place was obviously abandoned. The path to its gaping doorway was overgrown with weeds, and the big war galley moldered on the shore nearby, its sides staved in so that it couldn't be sailed. Instead, they followed the path through boggy ground toward the low, humped houses of the settlement. Maddie could see her relatives there pointing and calling each other. A crowd began to gather. The men unstrapped their packs and started taking out their wares. They were Travelers after all. There would be new things to see, and no one would die this day.

The last stranger lingered on the stepping-stones through the bog, studying the neglected castle. Maddie stared at his odd clothing and wondered where he came from. He was tall, and his face was lean and beardless—probably, she decided with feminine disdain, because he was too young to grow a beard. He looked, however, as if he might be somewhat handsome, and he had the appeal of being completely unknown. Curious and interested, she stepped into view, but as soon as the young man saw her, he turned away.

Feeling slightly disappointed, the girl retraced

her steps. She hurried up the steep, uneven stones of the spiral stairway and darted through the tower landing into the great room beyond. "Lady Mary," she called, "Travelers are here."

In the far corner of the dusty hall, gloomy with its few slit windows, a tall, bent old woman pushed away her embroidery frame and looked up from her work. Lady Mary inhabited one small part of the place just as a hen might nest in a tumbledown barn. Throughout the three floors of the castle were cobwebs, emptiness, and whispering echoes, but here in one corner of this great room were a gentlewoman's bed and furniture.

Leaving Lady Mary to consider these unexpected tidings, Maddie hurried back down the stairs, pulling a fold of her checkered blanket loose from her waist. She draped it around herself as a shawl and brought one long edge up to veil her hair. Picking her way across the stepping-stones, she followed the path the strangers had taken through the swampy ground by the loch.

On either side of the girl rose two lines of high hills, great, green undulating walls that defined the narrow valley. Just now their steep slopes were swathed in misty tatters of cloud. Trapped between those hills, like a long silver knife blade, lay the quiet waters of the loch, with the gray castle on its gravel shore and the flat, waterlogged bog land at its head.

The settlement lay beyond this bog on slightly higher ground, its fields spreading out around it and climbing the knees of the nearest hills. A small, shallow stream ran along its edge before vanishing into the bog and filtering into the loch. A dozen low turf houses, some longer and some shorter, were scattered across the muddy ground without any apparent pattern. Sheep and chickens wandered in and out of them, seeking their daily bread, and a few shaggy cattle grazed nearby.

Just now the little community was in a state of high excitement. The townspeople thronged the open land close to the bog to see what the Travelers had brought. Hooped milking buckets and harness ropes lay on the ground, along with fine silver knives and horn spoons. The old foreigner in breeches stood over a display of wooden ware: two-handled cups, butter makers, and small chests and boxes, their surfaces carved with complex patterns. Some diminutive saints stood on the grass beside them, their wooden faces serene.

Maddie spotted the beardless stranger again. He

had unslung his own pack and laid it by his feet, but he was carving rather than selling. He sat on a boulder a little distance away from the crowd, ignoring it completely. He was fashioning a figure with a thin, curved knife, shaving off a bit here and there.

The wood-carver was grown to a man's height, and his shoulders were broad, but Maddie doubted he could be much above her own age. There was a fragile quality to his hands as they turned the wood. They were bone-white, the fingers long and slender. There was a fragile quality, too, to the hunch of his lanky shoulders. Shaggy black hair fell into his face as he bent over his work. Maddie watched him for a long minute, but he never looked up.

A quiet belch at her elbow recalled the girl to her surroundings, and she glanced back to find the old man watching her indifferently. His wrinkled face was none too clean, and his cloth cap was unspeakable, but it was perhaps better than the long, grimy gray hair that it hid. "You don't see what you want," he proffered in a thick accent, "tell me, and the boy can make it."

Lady Mary was by Maddie's side now. The old woman had taken a few moments to augment her attire. A fine damask overdress covered her plain linen dress now, and her white hair was tucked into a dusty black velvet coif. Elegant in a way that their chief's own family had never been elegant, and dressed in a style that the local people had never understood, she commanded immediate attention from the strangers.

"And what would my lady like to see?" inquired the old man, leaning forward, his faded blue eyes suddenly greedy.

"This carving work," observed the woman. "It seems quite unusual."

"It is, it is," agreed the foreigner, stooping and retrieving a little box with alacrity. "He does handsome work, the boy does, whatever your heart can wish. This here," and he ran his greasy finger over the interlacing pattern on the box top, "this is the finest style. Tapestries ain't the taste anymore, carved paneling is the thing. Last year we worked for the Archbishop of Glasgow, carving panels to his study. He begged us not to leave, says he can't find any to match the work."

The regal woman considered this unlikely tale, her eyes, like Maddie's, on the young man in question. The wood-carver didn't look up to acknowledge their interest. He kept right on carving his figure as if he were the block of wood.

"But what am I to do," sighed Lady Mary, "an old woman in my rustic hermit's cell? I have no place for paneled walls."

"You have a chest that he can carve for you?" suggested the seller. "Or a box that he could work?" She nodded, her thin cheeks flushed, and the pair walked away from the crowd to make the bargain.

Maddie stood where they had left her, feeling jealous. A weaver's family was far from rich, and she couldn't even dream of owning carved chests. Then she saw something strange.

Sensing the pair's departure, or perhaps seeing their shadows move by him on the grass, the silent wood-carver glanced up quickly to study Lady Mary. His lean face was the color of bones, and his eyes were the clearest, brightest green. There was caution in those eyes—intelligence, too—and he stared after the old woman hungrily, as if he were learning her by heart. One long, penetrating glance, and he was working at his carving again as if he had never stopped.

The display of wooden ware was unattended, and the curious Maddie stepped close. "I can give you a linen kerchief for this one," she offered, pointing to a small, two-handled drinking cup. The peculiar young man didn't look at her. "Or maybe fifty," she continued, but he didn't appear to have heard.

"Can I see what you're making now?" she asked, walking over and stopping in front of him. "A tree? Why a tree? What is it for?" He didn't slow his work, the small, pale curls of wood falling onto his knees.

"Let me look at it," Maddie demanded, reaching down to take the carving from him. He didn't let it go, but he didn't look up, either. All she could see of him was black hair. "I want to buy it," she said stubbornly, trying to pull it away, but those white fingers had a firm grip on the little trunk.

"He don't ever speak, miss," warned a matter-of-fact voice, and she turned, blushing deeply, to find the disheveled old man by her side.

"Oh, I'm sorry," she exclaimed and started to step away, but those long fingers released the carving and left it in her hands. She turned it and stared at the intricate detail and lyrical expression that could make even a tiny fruit tree seem a beautiful, wonderful thing.

"You want that carving, miss?" asked the old man. He took it in his own hand and studied it dubiously. "A farthing for it, or its worth in goods." Maddie shook her head. She had no farthing or goods. A weaver's daughter couldn't come home with a useless statue. But what a canny little thing it was, to be sure. The regret showed on her face.

"Ah, now," he grunted, relenting, "tell me this. Who brews a strong drink here?"

"Little Ian makes the water of life."

"That's fine. Here's a groat. Just take this empty flask to him and have him fill it for me, and you can have the carving."

Maddie started off with a will, but curiosity overcame her. She quickly turned and looked back. The wood-carver was staring at her. She caught a swift impression of that extraordinary white face and those piercing green eyes before he dropped his head to stare at his hands. All that talent, and so sadly afflicted. What a tragedy. She walked off to find Little Ian.

The old man took advantage of a lull in the crowd's attention to turn to his prized craftsman.

"You carving trees out of trees now?" he asked perplexedly. "What's wrong with you, boy, you gone daft?"

But the strange wood-carver didn't answer a word. His attention was elsewhere. He was watching the girl make her way through the bystanders until she disappeared.

## 2

Maddie brought the filled flask back to the old man and hurried off with her carving across the muddy ground of the township. Every house in the community was one room wide and several rooms long, built of thick earthen walls and a heavy turf roof covered with brown heather thatch. Long weeds straggled across the older roofs. No house had windows, and the walls grew a friendly layer of grass and moss. They looked less like works of human architecture than animal dens, snug and safe against the winter storms. They had no chimneys, and the bluish smoke that rose from the peat fires burning within percolated out through the thatch roofs here and there like steam rising off the back of a cow.

Maddie reached her home. The two family sheep sprang from the doorway at her approach and scampered off. She ducked under the low door frame and stayed bent, keeping her head under the thickest layers of smoke.

Inside, the house was dark and quiet, warm and welcoming, smelling pleasantly of burning peat. A small fire of coals glowed in the hearth ring at the center of the dirt floor. After a short time, her eyes adjusted to the gloom and the haze of blue smoke. Furniture emerged from the darkness. The big box bed stood by an interior wall, its sides and top covered with boards to keep off grimy drops of moisture. Low stools grouped companionably by the hearth. Wicker boxes and the large wooden meal chest stood against the far wall. Wooden bowls and cups tumbled together on a shelf. Long sticks made a framework in the corner for the chickens to roost on at night, and a straw bed waited for the little brown sheep. The kettle on its long iron chain hung over the fire, and her mother's cooking utensils lay nearby. Fish and meat dangled from strings and hooks overhead, drying in the dense smoke, and above them, rising to a peak all but invisible in the darkness, lay the roof, its ceiling of long, thick sapling poles covered with soot. Even the spiderwebs that hung in shadowy profusion from the rafters were a shiny, sooty black.

Maddie's father, James, wove clothing and blankets for the community. His loom occupied an area at the lower end of the house, with its own door for light. But a wall separated it entirely from the main living room in order to reduce the smoke and soot. The family had to go out of doors and back in again to get to the weaving room.

Having seen nothing he needed from the Travelers' wares, James was at work again, singing as he threw the shuttle back and forth across the web of the loom. Maddie's mother, called Fair Sarah for her honey-colored hair, had seen several things she did need. Now Fair Sarah stood in the storeroom, considering what to trade. Maddie put the little carved tree on a shelf near the box bed and went to help her mother.

Maddie had spent almost every day of her life near this house, within sight of this tiny township, absorbed in the activities and accomplishments of her relations who farmed there. Every rise of ground and every rock was as familiar to her as the expressions on all the faces she knew so well. For the most part, the girl was content that this should be so. She would raise her own family within the beautiful green walls of the enfolding hills. She would return the care her parents had given her, place grandchildren in their laps, and close their eyes in their final sleep. Then her parents would lie peacefully beneath the moss of the old churchyard while she prayed for their souls in the little stone church. Her children would grow up to care for her, and the cycle of life would continue.

Only one detail of this pleasant picture still eluded the girl: a husband to help her father in the fields. The men of Maddie's settlement had fought hard for their defeated chief in the battles that had preceded her birth. Many lives had been lost, and in the downturn of the valley's fortunes, families had moved away. Widows were plentiful, but young men were scarce, and the few who remained didn't seem satisfactory. Maddie wasn't particularly worried, however. The problem of a husband would keep for another year or two, and perhaps the men would improve.

That night, Black Ewan feasted the Travelers at his big house so that they could tell their news and share their tales. The townspeople all came to enjoy the songs and stories, lining the long, smoky main room on benches or stools and spilling out into the cool night. The harvest would shortly be upon them, and they would soon be hard at work. They wouldn't have another such evening until the start of winter.

Maddie was there and gave out a song when bidden, but she looked in vain for the wood-carver. He wasn't sitting with the other strangers, and no one else seemed to have missed him. What would he be doing all by himself in the long summer twilight? Twilight was a dangerous time. Restless spirits and unholy beasts walked abroad until day. She worried about him as she listened to the tales.

"In a time not so far off, and in a valley not so far away, a group of boys went walking by the loch," said her uncle Colin the Smith. "All their kin had gone to Mass, but the day was hot, and they crept away together for a swim. No sooner had their feet touched the water than they saw a pretty sight. A white pony came trotting toward them along the shore.

"'Let's ride him!' proposed the oldest, and the others agreed. Only the littlest boy hung back.

"'He's not a horse,' the child protested, but the rest only laughed.

"They led the friendly pony over to a big rock, and they all began to climb on. Each boy found that there was room for him before they realized what was happening. The pony had stretched longer and longer in the middle until it looked like a big white lizard. 'Get off! Get off!' shrieked the littlest boy. 'I told you he's not a horse!'

"But now the boys discovered that they were stuck tight to the back of their mount. The strange pony threw back its pretty white head and laughed a long, loud horse's laugh.

"The little boy on the ground made the sign of the cross. In an instant, the illusion was gone. Instead of the pony, a great sea serpent thrashed on the shore of the loch. It dragged its screaming riders under the waves, and they were never seen again. They'd been taken by the Water Horse, shown for once in his own real shape."

The listeners nodded with satisfaction at this familiar story. Everyone who lived near water knew of the Water Horse. Usually he stayed deep below the surface of his home, the loch, but he watched for the unwary, appearing in pleasant disguises to lure them away. Once he trapped them, they couldn't escape. He pulled them into the water and gnawed the meat from their bones.

Maddie worried again about the wood-carver. He was a stranger to their country. Did he know to avoid the loch at night, when the shadow world came into its powers? Something about those green eyes made her keep thinking of him. He couldn't speak, but with such eyes, maybe he didn't need to.

As Maddie brought breakfast to Lady Mary in the castle the next morning, she saw the Travelers packing their ponies. By the time she came back, two of them were gone, but the carver and his grimy companion had stayed behind. The young man sat on a stone taking apart Lady Mary's box, and the old man was on his feet arguing with Father Mac.

The parish priest was a big, strong man with a thick neck and hands like slabs of beef. He was always out among the townspeople, working at the planting and harvesting or up on the roof mending thatch. It was said of him that he was one of the sons of a chief and could have had land and men for the asking, but he had run away instead to study Holy Writ.

"Father Mac?" Maddie had asked when she was a little girl. "Father MacWho?"

"Now, lass, that's a secret," he had told her gravely. "People should feel that their parish priest belongs to them, but the instant I tell my name, I have a whole set of friends and enemies. If I were Father Mackintosh or Father MacLeod, well, the Mackintosh and MacLean clans are at feud, and so are the MacLeods and the MacKenzies. Once, when I was studying with the bishop, another student heard my name and gave me a blow there and then. It isn't right for a priest to be scrapping like that. My hands are consecrated."

Crossing the boggy ground on the stepping stones, Maddie could hear the old Traveler's raised voice. "Thirty silver pennies, and not a penny less," he said in his funny accent. "Don't be saying you can't afford it, neither. I know about you clergies."

Father Mac spread his big hands apologetically. "I could never raise such a sum for a new Madonna for our church. But our old statue isn't anything to match his talent, and the whole parish would be grateful. It would be a good deed, something to help him in the hereafter."

"Hereafter?" scoffed the Traveler. "That don't mean a thing to him. He don't got a hereafter."

As Father Mac framed a philosophical response to this, he caught sight of the approaching girl. "Good morning, young Madeleine," he rumbled. "How are your parents this fine day?"

"Both well, Father," she answered. "Dad hopes you'll have a chess game with him tonight."

"Willingly," said the priest. "Tell him I'll come once the lamps are lit. I'm Father Mac," he told the Traveler, extending his hand.

"Ned," rejoined the old man, shaking hands with the priest. "Thirty pennies for the statue," he repeated, to show that the handshake wouldn't help.

"What's his name?" asked Maddie, pointing at the young man busy with his carving work.

"He don't got a name," answered Ned with a shrug. "What does he need with one?"

A few days later, Maddie slowed her walk up from the old castle, where she had delivered Lady Mary's breakfast. She was enjoying the lovely morning. The sky was a deep, clear blue, and the loch was sparkling. The sun had climbed over the rim of the hills to the east, filling the valley with shades of green and turning the grain fields gold. Purple heather bloomed on the hillsides, looking rusty brown in the distance.

Near the path from the castle were several great gray boulders, sunk waist-deep in the mud and moss. The wood-carver was sitting on one of these, his tools spread out around him and the top panel of Lady Mary's box across his knees. But he wasn't doing his work. He was looking at the high hills that rose in jagged walls along either side of the valley. For the last several days, the low clouds had covered them completely.

Maddie walked quietly up behind the young man and stood beside the boulder, looking over his shoulder at his carving. On the flat box panel, leafy vines stretched and twined in complex knots, curving over and under one another like her father's checkered weaving patterns. As soon as he realized she was there, the carver fell to work again, reaching for a thin chisel.

"This line of hills on this side, we call them the Green Hills," she told him, just as if he had asked her. "And the hills over there are the Black Hills because the pine woods look black when it rains. No one knows why the Green Hills don't have any woods on them, but they don't, and Little Ian says that if you plant a tree there it will die."

The mysterious young man glanced up at the hills as she spoke, and she gathered courage.

"That peak there," she said, pointing, "that's the Old Woman. Now is the only time of year she doesn't wear her kerchief of snow. And the peak right in front of us, where the two ridges meet and the valley ends, that's the Herdsman. All the clouds come to the Herdsman, and then they stop and rain because they can't get away." The wood-carver looked from peak to peak as she pointed, his white face thoughtful and interested.

"Our town is called the Chief's Home, and the castle by the loch is called the Chief's House because our chief used to live there. But before I was born, the new lord came to take the land. Our men turned out for the chief, but he lost in the fighting and went away. The battles went on for years, and we fought for him every time he tried to come back. He's dead now. The new lord put Lady Mary in the castle. We think she's kin to the new lord's wife, but she doesn't ever say."

The young man turned on his boulder to look back at the abandoned castle, its stark, square form rising from the shore of the loch, its tower doorway gaping and empty, and its paths covered over in grass. Long black smears of mildew stained the gray walls, a bleak sight on that lovely day. So the carver knew her language after all, decided Maddie, even though his clothes were so strange. Father Mac said breeches were English.

"Would you like a piece of bannock?" she asked, reaching into her basket. "My mother just made it."

Immediately the spell was broken, or maybe the spell resumed. The wood-carver went back to work, his face hidden behind his hair. Maddie stood there for a little while, watching the wood shavings lift before the chisel blade. At last she sighed and walked away, leaving part of an oatcake on the boulder beside him.

Some time later, Black Ewan walked by the boulder, and he, too, studied the carving, but he was not as impressed with the delicate work as the friendly girl had been. Harvesttime was here, and the harvest was good, but they lacked the hands to gather it. He could remember when there had been enough men to bring in the harvest and row the big war galley, too. Now widows did the work of the men who had fallen in battle.

Black Ewan had the running of his dead brother's house, lands, and herds, with his brother's widow and her two children to look after and the three men who worked his fields to command. He was the most important farmer in the settlement, and he ran most things there, seeing that the other widows and their children worked hard and didn't go hungry. He was both fair and good to them, but he brooded in the evenings over the lost pride and hope of his youth.

Black Ewan had been named for his black hair, but the name was a good match to his temper. He had stayed by his chief and wandered with him through long, uncertain years, hiding, organizing the men for battle, hoping for victory, and finally bringing his fallen leader's body home to rest with his fathers when hope was gone at last. Black Ewan had returned after all that time to find everything changed. A stranger woman lived in his dead chief's castle. His sweetheart worked for that woman, and she didn't want to marry him anymore. Perhaps she just thought herself too old for marriage, but he blamed Lady Mary. His sweetheart had sickened and died years ago, but he still didn't forget. He had heard new sermons during his wandering years, words full of righteousness and rigor. He was far more interested in the Old Law, with its eye given for an eye, than he was in Father Mac's sermons of compassion and love.

Now he looked at the carving and clenched his fists in anger. "There are tools to mend and the barley to cut!" he roared. "And you waste your time carving leaves for that worthless woman who won't spin a thread for her keep!"

He smacked the board, sending it flying out of the young man's grasp. But the wood-carver sat just like wood himself, not moving a muscle. The farmer relented at the sight.

"God has already struck the boy," muttered Black Ewan. "It isn't right that I should." He walked away to talk with Little Ian.

The young man watched the retreating figure cautiously through the locks of his own black hair. As soon as the farmer disappeared, he gathered up his carving tools and headed toward the nearest range of hills.

It was most unfortunate, considering Black Ewan's state of mind, that the next person he should come across was the wood-carver's companion. Old Ned lay on the ground at the edge of the settlement, his head propped on a small stone, watching the sunlight fall through the twirling leaves of a birch tree. In his clasped hands, he held his half-empty flask, and he was perfectly at peace with the world.

"Widows are in the fields doing a man's work," said Black Ewan severely. "And you lie here doing nothing at all!"

"Looks like it," affirmed the Traveler without remorse, raising the flask to his lips.

"No man should eat his bread in idleness," growled the farmer, standing over him.

"Bread," grunted the old man in contempt. "You people don't know what bread is."

"You mean to lie about in drunken sloth while other folk bring in your food," snapped Black Ewan. "Your simpleminded boy earns your keep."

"He likes his work," agreed the reprobate, "but work don't appeal to me. Each to his strength, says I."

God didn't appear to have struck this old man, so Black Ewan gladly did it for Him. He yanked the Traveler to his feet, pounded him well, and dragged him off by the back of his tunic, bleeding and cursing.

"You'll work a harvest for once in your life," he declared, shoving the old man along. "I have the perfect companion for a sodden blasphemer like you." They came to the edge of the grain fields. Here the townspeople had erected a chest-high fence, or dyke, of cut turf blocks. "Angus," announced the farmer, coming through a gap in the earthen dyke, "here's someone to help with the herding."

A band of small, shaggy black cows grazed beside the dyke, moving slowly and impassively within their whining cloud of gnats and midges, their short horns sweeping outward and their long hair falling over their eyes. Leaning against the grassy dyke and watching them was an awesome giant of a man, with matted hair falling into his eyes and a cloud of midges all his own. An aged and stained blanket, haphazardly wrapped, was the only clothing he wore.

Once, Angus had been his chief's proudest warrior, the champion of the castle, but he had returned from battle and exile to find his wife and children dead. He had roamed the winter hills in despair, trying to extinguish in his colossal body the life that he no longer wanted to live. High fever and sickness had followed, and it seemed his wish would be granted. But the powerful body lived on. It was the mind that died.

Angus blundered about like a great bull, and, like a bull, he had to be tamed. Colin the Smith made one of the iron kettle chains into a fetter for him and found the key to the old padlock that had once locked up the chief's prisoners. By day, the giant shuffled about on simple tasks, his long legs chained together to keep him from running off into the hills. By night, he slept in Black Ewan's house in an empty cattle stall, his head pillowed on hay and his leg chained to the wall.

Now Angus stared mildly up at his keeper as Black Ewan dropped the bleeding Traveler onto the grass beside him. Pulling the big key from around his neck, the farmer unfastened the padlock and locked one fetter around the Traveler's leg instead, chaining the two men together at the ankle.

"There," he remarked, putting the key around his neck again. "This work isn't too hard for an old man like you. Just chase the cattle if they start to break into the grain fields, and bellow if anything goes wrong. Watch Angus if you're not sure; he'll soon teach you what to do." And he went off to his work again, listening with pleasure to the stream of frantic curses that followed him over the dyke.

# 3

Maddie had just taken supper to Lady Mary in the castle, and now she was looking forward to her own meal. She stepped out of the tower into the clear light of a summer evening, studying the silhouettes of the great birds flying down to the loch.

"Madeleine!" called a low voice. She turned to find the wood-carver standing there. He was staring straight at her with those piercing green eyes, and her heart skipped a beat.

"I didn't know you could talk!" she said in delight. "It's Maddie, though; only Father Mac calls me Madeleine."

The carver looked around cautiously and stepped closer. "Help me find Ned," he said in a husky whisper. "I've searched for him everywhere."

"The old man's chained up with Mad Angus. He and Black Ewan had a fight."

"Chained up!" exclaimed the young man. "He can't be chained up! When will he be free?"

"Probably in a few weeks," Maddie answered. "Dad said Black Ewan said after the harvest."

"But what am I going to do?" he asked, looking stunned. "Can we free him somehow?"

"What, take the key from Black Ewan?" She laughed. "It's a little beyond us, I'd say. He'd knock me silly, for a start, and it's more than your life's even worth."

"More than my life's worth," muttered the young man. "That's not much." He stood for a minute looking around at the castle, the loch, the far hills. If he sought inspiration, he didn't find any. He looked at her again, hopeless and frustrated. Then he walked away.

"Where are you going?" demanded the mystified girl, but he didn't answer. By the time she could follow, he was well ahead of her. She watched him walk off into the distance, taking the path along the shore of the loch.

Maddie fell asleep thinking of the good-looking carver boy. If he had been remarkable before, he was close to perfect now. His speech wasn't foreign, like that of the drunken Englishman. He spoke just like she did. Maybe he'd been stolen from his cradle by the wandering Travelers, and that was why he wasn't like Ned. He might be a nobleman by birth. He might even be the son of a chief.

But if Maddie's thoughts were pleasant ones, her dreams were dark and grim. She wandered through her town as thunder rumbled in the swollen clouds above, and not one living person did she find. The houses were silent and abandoned, their belongings tossed about. Filth covered the dirt floors, and some of the roofs had fallen in. Everywhere was the smell of decay.

Strewn across the weedy ground between the houses lay an untidy mosaic of bones. They glimmered white and phosphorescent in the dim twilight of the storm. Flesh still clung to some, dried and blackened. So many were underfoot that she couldn't help stepping on them.

The little parish church was completely destroyed, the rock walls torn apart. Gravestones were tossed aside and graves dug open, to let something in—or to let it out. Not a single creature moved in that ghastly land of death. The only sound was the sighing of the wind and the ominous growling of the thunder.

The girl stood bewildered in the middle of her town. What could have accomplished this destruction? Human raiders would never have dug up the churchyard. Animals wouldn't have left the bones behind. Some evil of the ancient world had descended upon this place, a thing that kept both people and animals away. Maddie froze, caught by an abrupt foreboding. That thing was still here.

An enemy stalked the vacant houses and corpse-littered ground, hunting her as its prey. She saw nothing, heard nothing beyond the empty rush of wind. But the air grew cold, and then very cold. A black shadow fell over her.

Maddie sat bolt upright in the box bed, her heart pounding wildly. Her mother and father slept peacefully beside her, and her town was not a welter of bones. Bright moonlight poured into the room through the open doorway, and perfect stillness reigned outside. But the room was freezing cold, colder than the bitter nights of winter, and Maddie felt a hideous presence. The enemy had not stayed behind in her nightmare. It had followed her here.

A low murmuring came to her, a hissing, bubbling, muttering sound from the back wall of the house. Slowly it passed along the windowless wall, and she followed the noise to the storeroom. The muttering thing was moving around the end of the house. It was coming toward the open doorway.

Teeth chattering, Maddie made the sign of the cross and knelt by the hearth in the middle of the room. Shutting the door wouldn't help. It was nothing but a wickerwork panel covered with hide. Waking her parents wouldn't help, either. The thing was almost here. She scraped the ashes of the hearth, hoping to find a friendly spark underneath, but the peat coals had been bedded for the night and would need coaxing to come back to life. Like a hare in a trap, she stared at the moonlit square of the open doorway, the only way out of the house. Her hands fumbled over the hearthstones and found her mother's bannock spade.

Colin the Smith had made his sister a spatula of iron to turn the oatcakes on the hearth. Its wooden handle felt solid in Maddie's hand, and its thin, heart-shaped wedge came to a point. It wasn't a knife, but it was a weapon of sorts, and Maddie felt glad of it. She clutched it and listened as the bubbling sounds came nearer.

The square of moonlight vanished into inky blackness as a shape moved in front of the door. Maddie prayed for her life and hurled the iron weapon. A sound burst from the thing, a loud whistling shriek. When she opened her eyes, that great black shape was gone.

"What is it?" demanded her father, scrambling up from the bed, and then Fair Sarah's arms were around her.

"Something outside," she whimpered, hugging her mother. "Something big at the door. It hissed."

"I'll go see," decided James Weaver, reaching for his knife. Then he froze right where he was. Maddie stopped in the middle of a word, and her mother's arms gripped her tightly.

A weeping, worrying sound rose into the night from somewhere very close. It keened and whined, gaining strength, until it became a scream, wavering in the air while time stood still. As it faded away, the three huddled together, clinging to one another for support.

"I'll just—just—go see," stammered her father, holding the knife in trembling hands.

"Jamie," sobbed his wife, "oh, Jamie, don't go out there."

A shadow fell across the doorway again, and Maddie gave a gasp. "James," called Black Ewan's voice, "is all well with you?"

"Yes," answered the weaver, shaking off his family. He wrapped his woolen blanket around his waist and shoulders, and he and the farmer walked away into the moonlight. Maddie and her mother heard the voices of neighbors calling from house to house, the bawling of cattle, and the wailing of children.

Fair Sarah knelt by the hearth and built the fire, whispering over the spent coals the morning prayer to the Trinity. The frightened girl followed her lead, starting her chores, and the night began to brighten into the dim gray of early dawn.

They heard the men coming back, talking loudly, their voices strained and excited. "Did you find it?" demanded Fair Sarah anxiously, going to the door. "What was it? Did it get away?"

The men came up to the house. Black Ewan and Colin the Smith were carrying something heavy, but Maddie couldn't see what it was.

"It got away," said her father. "We don't know where it went. But it found that young wood-carver on the path near the castle, and we don't know if he's going to live."

# 4

They brought the wood-carver into the house and laid him on the floor by the hearth. Maddie couldn't even see him for the crowd around him.

"His shirt's in ribbons."

"Look at those claw marks! That's a big animal. It stood up to attack. The wounds start at the shoulder."

"I can't believe a claw could do that. They're as neat as knife cuts."

"He's burning up with fever."

"Maddie, run fetch water." That was her mother's voice. Maddie snatched up the wooden pail, edged her way to the door, and ran across the wet grass to the little stream. When she came back, most of the neighbors were gone, checking on their livestock or hunting the attacker. Maddie ducked under the low door frame and stepped into the room to find Fair Sarah and Father Mac kneeling by the unconscious young man and sewing him up industriously.

"Find a needle, lass," boomed Father Mac. "There's work for everyone. No, no, I'm only joking," he added as her mother looked up in concern.

Maddie set down the pail of water and looked at the object of their handiwork. The wood-carver lay on his back, his blood-soaked tunic in a ball beside him. Long red wounds raked diagonally across his pale chest, clustered in lines of four. Bright blood still ran from them and dripped down onto the dirt floor. Her mother kept dabbing the wounds with the tattered tunic so she could see where to stitch.

"It's not as bad as it looks," said Father Mac. "Most of the cuts are shallow. The deepest one is this gash here on the arm. Probably he threw a hand up to defend himself and caught the full force of a claw."

"It's not the wounds, it's the fever that worries

me," confessed Fair Sarah. "He's as pale as flax from the blood loss, but he's blazing with heat. And to take a fever so quick after an injury!"

Father Mac nodded in agreement. "Aye, that has me puzzled, too," he rumbled. "It's uncanny all the way around."

Maddie knelt down by them, her attention caught by a faint line under the slashes. She traced a semicircle of scars making its dim purple track across the wounded shoulder.

"He's been mauled before," observed the priest. "That's some kind of bite. It's a risk of the traveling life, I suppose, but nothing like this attack."

"Did you know he can talk?" asked Maddie. "Not like that old man he travels with—he talks just like us."

"So he's one of our own folk," mused Father Mac. "I suspected as much from his craft. He's no coward, either; he faced the intruder fair and square. There isn't a single claw mark on his back."

The pair stitched and bandaged while Maddie made breakfast and hurried through the gray morning to take the meal to Lady Mary. All the men were out, urging on Black Ewan's pair of dogs. They had already been through the castle with torches, but they hadn't found anything. Lady Mary was supremely annoyed at their intrusion.

"The wood-carver is badly injured," Maddie told her, spooning the porridge from her wooden bowl into Lady Mary's silver one. "They don't know what attacked him."

"You're late," answered the contrary woman. "I can tell your mother didn't cook this egg." And she pretended not to be interested in the news.

By the time Maddie returned, Father Mac and Fair Sarah were finished. They had brought the settle out of the storeroom and moved it to the wall by the door, making it into a bed for the wood-carver. The settle was long, like a bench, but it had a wooden back like a chair. The injured young man lay on it with his eyes closed, wrapped in a blanket and not moving at all.

"Fresh bloodstains," said her mother briskly, picking up the shredded tunic. "He'll not wear this again, so we've no need to waste salt drawing the stain. Cold water will take out most of it. Maddie, do you take this to the stream and wash it well. We'll use it for more bandages. He'll be needing them, I'm afraid."

Going out with the tunic, Maddie stumbled over

something and spied the bannock spade lying at her feet. She picked it up and hefted it, remembering the feel of it in her hand. A smear marred the tip of the iron, and Maddie rubbed it. Nothing. She licked her finger and rubbed again. There was blood on her finger now.

"Black Ewan, Dad," she called, coming over to the men, and she showed them the bannock spade. She told them what had happened while they passed the tool from hand to hand.

"It came around from the back of the house," Black Ewan said. "Around which way?"

"Past the storeroom," she answered.

"Against the sun," observed Little Ian, his sharp fox's face sharper with excitement. "The wrong direction. It's an evil spirit."

"That's why the dogs aren't picking up a scent," said Gillies, one of Black Ewan's farmhands. "They keep running around in circles. They can't find anything at all."

"But what about the blood?" asked Maddie's father. "Spirits don't bleed."

"It must be the Water Horse," suggested Little Ian, "and she drove it away with the holy metal."

"The Water Horse here among our houses!"

exclaimed the smith. "It'll drag us all down into the loch."

The townspeople couldn't do much to defend themselves against the Water Horse. Strong doors they didn't have, nor city walls with gates. But they pulled the big, cumbersome swords and battle-axes out of the storerooms and made sure they had an edge, and Father Mac went from house to house, blessing the hearths with holy water. At noon the priest led a solemn procession around the perimeter of the town, and then the people went back to work on the harvest, feeling that they had done what they could. As they worked, they mused over the disquieting event. The Water Horse didn't often come among human dwellings. Some evil was drawing it close.

Maddie ran errands to the fields all afternoon. Off and on, as she hurried by her house, she stopped inside the doorway to look at the unconscious woodcarver. She wanted him to open his eyes and tell her what had happened, but he didn't move all day.

Walking back bone-tired in the evening, she saw her pretty cousin Bess sitting on top of the wall of her uncle's house. Bess was the daughter of Colin the Smith, and she and Maddie were the same age, but whereas Maddie was her parents' only child, Bess was the oldest of seven.

The thatch on the smith's house was old, and green weeds grew abundantly over it. The family's two milking sheep were grazing on the roof, with a string tied to a back leg of each so they couldn't jump away in a panic and tumble to the ground. The string was tied to Bess's belt, leaving her hands free to spin thread.

Bess's distaff was a thick wooden rod a couple of feet long, covered with loosely wrapped wool fibers. She held the distaff tucked under one arm, pulling fibers from it into a long strand. The other end of the strand was attached to a short stick weighted with a stone ring, a spindle. Bess dropped this spindle, twirling it, and it twisted the fibers into a thread. Then she wound the thread around the little spindle and pulled more wool loose from the distaff, keeping the chain of fibers from one to the other even, so that the thread would not break.

"Daddy says it's a shame that the Water Horse attacked that poor carver boy," said Bess. "Daddy says he's just a harmless halfwit."

Maddie clambered up to sit beside her cousin on the low house wall. "He's not a halfwit," she said with a frown.

Bess dropped her spindle, giving it a deft twirl. She and Maddie had been spinning thread for years. It was one of the most important activities women did, and they did it whenever and wherever they could.

"He doesn't even know how to talk," she retorted.

"He can talk," countered Maddie. "He talked to me last night, but he was afraid someone would see him. The old man probably beats him when he talks."

"Why would anyone do that?" Bess wanted to know, hauling on the strings to pull the sheep back from the house ridge. The small brown sheep always wanted to eat whatever was out of reach.

"Father Mac said he probably doesn't want the boy to sell his own carvings. Otherwise, he'd keep the goods for himself, and then the drunkard couldn't afford his drink, and serve him right."

"You should have seen the old man this morning with the cattle," chuckled Bess. "Mad Angus was trotting back and forth just like he always does, and he was stumbling along after him and cursing until he was hoarse. I brought the children out to watch, and they had such fun they didn't give me a bit of trouble the whole time."

"The poor carver hasn't opened his eyes all day," Maddie said. "I wonder what he was doing out so early. The Travelers were staying in the bottom level of the castle, but Dad said he was on the path right by the houses."

"Maybe he saw that you were in danger," suggested Bess. "He must have seen the Water Horse at your house and run out of the castle to fight it. It probably screamed because he stabbed it and saved your life."

Maddie was thrilled. "Do you really think he fought a monster for me? He couldn't have killed it. They didn't find the body."

"Then it crawled away to die," declared Bess, with the air of one who has an answer for anything. "I'll bet it crawled back into the loch and sank right to the bottom."

The next morning was windy and cloudy. Maddie's parents were both out in the fields, but Fair Sarah had told the girl to stay at home so she could keep an eye on the sick wood-carver. He tossed and turned in delirium, muttering strange sentences and crying out in pain. Maddie brought her work and sat by him, putting wet rags on his head, but the fever was so high that the rags dried out almost at once. When Fair Sarah came home to check on him, she couldn't think what else to do. She was sure they were losing the fight.

"Do you fetch Lady Mary," she decided. "She'll know something to help him."

If Lady Mary had been their real kin, the townspeople never would have minded the keeping of her, and even if she had acted like a normal old woman, they wouldn't have minded her then. But she wouldn't spin thread or watch the little ones while their parents did the work, and she didn't cook dinner for them when they labored in the fields. They had to cook for her. She didn't even walk among them if she could help it, and she never once came into the church. She just sat in her great, gloomy hall day and night and read books or worked on her embroidery.

The only thing that Lady Mary did do for the townspeople was curing the sick and the injured, and Maddie tended a patch of healing herbs for her up on the hillside. But of all the strange things about Lady Mary, this was the strangest. She always seemed to know just how to cure an illness, and that was white witchcraft. If she could cure, she could probably harm, too. That was black witchcraft.

Lady Mary stepped into the weaver's house and knelt down by the settle to examine the carver. "His fever is very high," she reported, "but there is no flush to his cheeks. A poison is locked deep inside his chest, drying up his blood. The element of water must counteract the dry fire, or soon water and wood will be consumed, and only earth will remain. I'll make you a mixture of herbs to brew and pour down his throat. Force him to drink as much water as you can. It will push the poison out through the skin and restore a balance to the humors of the body. Once it begins to work and you see him perspiring, keep the fire hot and pile blankets on him. Change the bedding frequently and wash it in clear water to dissipate the poisonous exudations."

"I knew you would know what to do," sighed Fair Sarah in relief.

That night they kept the peat fire burning hotly and didn't bank it with ash. Maddie curled up in the box bed, listening to the wood-carver groan and mutter. But she woke the next morning to hear her mother talking to him, and over breakfast, Fair Sarah was elated.

"Lady Mary's brew is working wonderfully!" she whispered to them while the young man slept. "His fever is down, and he's in his own mind. I'm calling him Carver."

"And he's talking, Sarah?" inquired the weaver before Maddie could ask the same question.

"Well, no," admitted his wife. "He's back to his old tricks. But he drank his brew and a big mug of water when I asked him to."

Maddie hurried off to morning Mass and delivered Lady Mary's breakfast. Then she hunted for eggs, took water to the reapers in the grain fields, and gathered sheep's wool. The sheep were shedding their thick winter coats, rubbing the wool off on trees and stones. She filled two egg-shaped wicker baskets with wool and carried them back to the house. She laid more peat blocks on the fire and tiptoed over to the settle to check on Carver.

The young man was pale and sweaty, buried under blankets, and his black hair was sticking to his temples. He caught a glimpse of her and quickly looked away. Then he turned and stared.

"Madeleine!" he gasped.

"It's Maddie," she reminded him. The old hen with the bent comb was roosting on his blankets. She cackled loudly in protest when Maddie shooed her off.

"Madeleine, what are you doing here?" he demanded in a whisper.

"I live here," she told him. "That was my ma you wouldn't talk to this morning. Why won't you talk to her? You talk to me."

The wood-carver glanced around the empty room, his eyes dull and tired. His face was leaner than before, and there were big black rings under his eyes. He looked like he was suffering, decided Maddie, probably because he was. He glanced back at her and made an effort to move his head closer to her.

"What did I do?" he asked in a low voice. She looked puzzled. "To get here," he explained urgently. "What did I do? You'll have to tell me because I can't remember."

"You saved my life," said Maddie, and she smiled at him. Perhaps she was no beauty, but her straight hair had russet highlights, and her brown eyes were soft and pretty. The young man gazed at her, and the suffering look on his face eased. But just for a short space of time. Then it was back.

"From what?" he muttered. When she gave him a blank look, he gritted his teeth. "Saved you from what?" he insisted doggedly.

Maddie told him about her narrow escape from the Water Horse and his leaving the castle to save her. Then she described the various searches they had organized and the town defenses against the beast. During the whole spirited rendition, the woodcarver stared up at the sooty, cobweb-hung ceiling, his face wearing no expression whatsoever.

"So it came here," he murmured. "Straight to your house. You were the first person it wanted to kill."

Maddie watched him in silence for a minute, so full of questions that she didn't know where to start. "Who are your people?" she wanted to know. But he didn't answer her.

"Is Carver what your own people call you?" she persisted. "Why do you travel with a foreigner? Why doesn't he know your name?" The young man closed his eyes, and she wasn't sure he was listening anymore. "Carver's what we'll call you if you can't tell us something better. But don't you want us to call you by your name?"

"No," he whispered. "I don't have a name anymore." And he pretended to sleep until she gave up asking questions and walked away.

That night, Maddie dreamed that the young wood-carver was walking through her town. His face was very white, but the shadow at his feet was sooty black, as black as a hole in the ground. He stopped, but the shadow didn't want to stand still with him. It flickered like a dark flame, as if it longed to tear itself free, and all the green grass that fell under it turned dry and brittle. She stepped closer, leaning down to look at it, and the black form on the ground gave a long, shuddering hiss.

Maddie woke and sat up in the darkness with the hiss still in her ears, remembering the enemy standing at her door. But this time it wasn't a hiss she heard. The sick wood-carver was talking in his sleep. She dozed off again, listening to the soft whispers repeating over and over, like a song without a tune.

5

The next morning, as Maddie hunted for eggs, she heard a gruff voice hailing her. The Traveler was limping along by Angus. "Hey!" he called. "How's the lad?" Maddie reluctantly came over.

"Carver's getting better," she reported coldly. "The fever is gone, but he's too weak to be up yet. He was badly wounded."

The old man gave a noncommittal grunt. "Wounded how?" he asked. "The farmhands was talking nonsense over some big bogey from the loch."

"It was an animal with claws. It slashed him across the chest, so—and so—and so, like that," she explained, mimicking the long strokes over her own front.

Ned chuckled. "Yeah, like that," he agreed with a grin. Maddie frowned. "The lad talking yet?" he continued, and that put her in mind of all those beatings he must have given out. She glared wholeheartedly at him. The blackguard had no feelings at all.

"You told me yourself that he never speaks," she snapped.

"Bless me if you ain't keeping secrets for him already! Do Ned a favor," he proposed, fishing out a grimy coin. "Run and bring a mouthful of that water of life. Ah, come on," he coaxed as she looked disgusted. "The boy would want you to. Fetch old Ned a bit to live on while I'm dragged around."

Maddie marched over to Little Ian's house and found his wife at home. "Here," she said shortly, holding out the penny, "the old felon in chains wants a drop."

The woman was just stirring the morning porridge. She took the penny. "If Black Ewan keeps him through the harvest like he plans," she remarked, "this may be the first year that we pay our rent in coins."

Carver slept most of the next several days, the fever, wounds, and blood loss having left him in a state of apathetic weakness. He rarely spoke, and his hands shook so much that he could hardly feed himself.

"Madeleine," he called one morning as she walked by. "Where are my carving tools?"

"Goodness," answered Maddie, "I don't know. I suppose they're wherever you left them."

"In the castle," he whispered, stirring restlessly under the blankets. "That was days ago. They might be stolen."

"No one steals around here," said Maddie with a smile. "Everyone would know about it." But the young man still looked worried.

"Could you bring them to me?" he asked. "They're on a shelf in the back corner, rolled up in a leather holder. I hate not having them. I need them. I need to carve."

"I'll fetch them," promised the girl, "but you can't carve yet. Look at you! You can barely hold a spoon."

The young man's eyes were beseeching. "But I do carve when I'm like this," he whispered earnestly. "I have to, it's the only thing I like to do."

Maddie took a long look at that suffering face

and felt profoundly sad. "I'll go get your knives," she said, "and I'll ask my ma. Maybe she'll let you carve."

Fair Sarah was shocked at the idea. "He still needs rest," she told her daughter. "He doesn't need to worry about working yet."

"I don't think he's worried about working," mused Maddie. "I think he's worried about resting."

Maddie's mother soon found this out for herself. That evening she shook wood shavings out of her silent patient's blankets and looked around the bare room in astonishment. One knob on the back of the wooden settle had blossomed into a pale, many-petaled rose.

The family ate their meals sitting on low stools by the hearth, and before too many days, Carver was well enough to join them. Wrapped in his blanket, eyes on his bowl, he listened to the banter that went on around him. He still wouldn't speak to anyone but Maddie, his voice low and cautious, so Maddie began to speak for him, as if he were a very small child.

"Carver wants more porridge," she would announce when his bowl was empty.

"Of course he can have it," her mother would reply, and the young man would hold out his bowl for another spoonful.

One day, Maddie hit upon the ingenious device of lying about his wishes. "Carver hates this soup," she declared matter-of-factly. "He won't eat it."

"That's—that's not true," stammered the wood-carver, caught off-guard. "I think—I think it's very good." He shot Maddie a reproachful glance, and she gave him a triumphant grin.

Maddie's mother spent as much time as she could spare tending to her patient, and she spent more time than that worrying about him. Concerned over his obsessive carving, she asked Maddie to borrow Lady Mary's beautiful playing cards. Maddie spent a few minutes teaching the invalid how to play and left him busy with the cards as she went about her duties. But when she returned, she found he had abandoned the game. He was back at his carving.

"What happened?" she demanded. "Did you forget how it went?"

"No," muttered the young man without looking up. "The cards don't like me."

"They don't like you?" exclaimed Maddie, laughing. "Are you upset that you lost?"

Carver was nettled. "It's not that I lost. I'll show you," he said, setting aside his tools and looking around to make sure no one else was there. He shuffled the deck as well as he could and laid out the first four cards.

They were the King and Knave of Swords, followed by the King and Knave of Clubs. Maddie stared at the armed figures in surprise.

"See how angry they are," said the wood-carver in a low voice. "They'd come at me if they could. Don't ask me to play that game anymore. The cards know things."

But if the mysterious young man didn't like card games, he soon developed an interest in chess. Father Mac and the weaver often had a game after sundown, bending over Father Mac's chessboard in the flickering light of a rush lamp. As long as he was bedridden, Carver pretended to sleep through the visits. He told Maddie that he didn't trust priests.

"There weren't any priests in my town," he said, "and my mother said that was a good thing. She came from fisher folk, and they know priests are dangerous. They hex the nets and cause storms at sea. She said a man who took a priest in his boat would surely die because the sea gods would drown him."

Maddie chuckled. "I never heard anything so silly. Priests aren't dangerous."

"Anyway, we didn't need them," insisted Carver.

"If we needed something, my mother would pray and kill a chicken and watch the birds that came to eat its insides. Then she knew what was going to happen."

"That sounds like nonsense, too," commented the girl. "Father Mac says no one knows the future. You can trust a priest like him. He's the servant of God, the One True God, and there aren't any other gods."

The young man looked unconvinced. "Maybe not on land," he muttered.

The first time Father Mac came over after Carver was well enough to be up, the invalid was plainly uncomfortable about it. He sat hunched on a stool, fidgeting with his hands. An uneasy silence settled over the room.

"Son, I was hoping you'd help me," remarked Father Mac. "I've cut a new staff, and it's not to my liking. You see, when I put my hand here, this knot catches my palm."

The task soothed the young man's nerves like magic. He sat beside the two men, smoothing and shaping the wood, and Father Mac did him the kindness of ignoring him completely. Maddie glanced up from her spinning after a few minutes to find him cutting a decorative band of diamonds into the staff.

As the game went on, Carver began to pay less attention to his project and more attention to the chessboard. He picked up a captured pawn and turned it thoughtfully in his fingers, evaluating the clumsy woodwork. Quietly and calmly, Father Mac began to explain the game as they played. By the end, the young man was interested enough to ask questions.

"James, I'd better go," announced the priest, reaching for his staff. The wood-carver gave a guilty start.

"I'm sorry," he muttered, handing it over. "I didn't finish it."

"Ah, well," said Father Mac with a smile, "there's always tomorrow night."

Every house had to be supplied with its fuel to feed the hearth fires during the long months of winter. The small bricks of dark brown peat, cut out of the bogs in early summer, were dry and ready to be brought home. Maddie and Bess worked long days lugging the peats to the houses and building them up into round stacks. Well enough to walk now, Carver began to help them.

The two girls made their way home with heavy baskets slung across their backs, leaning forward against the pull of the headbands that helped them manage the baskets' weight. They talked and laughed, spinning thread as they walked along, and the silent young man followed them with a half-loaded basket of his own, listening to their songs and carefree chatter. He almost looked like one of them now in the new shirt Fair Sarah had made him and one of her long sheepskin blankets wrapped around his shoulders and waist. He persisted in wearing his woolen breeches, though, and Bess thought that was funny. All the other men she knew went about with their legs bare below their knee-length shirts. Although he wore a much longer shirt, even Father Mac didn't wear breeches.

In the evenings, the young man sat by the weaver's fire mending harvest tools. He had set aside Lady Mary's box without finishing it, and that woman was not happy with him.

"I already paid him half the price for the work," she complained to Maddie one morning, looking out a narrow window at the gray day outside. She rarely left her dusty room. Maddie didn't know how she could stand it.

"But it's harvesttime," pointed out the girl, tidying stacks of books. "And the tools break so often. Carver says in the south they make them out of iron."

"I'm the one who paid," snapped the old woman. "It's little enough I have now."

Maddie looked at the elegant furniture in the corner of that great, gloomy hall and felt in her heart that Lady Mary was right. Once, the new lord's wife had visited her every few months, bringing presents and sweetmeats. Later, she had sent her servants to the old woman with those comforts that the rich needed to have: new embroidery canvas and thread, furs and muffs, and pieces of lovely cloth.

But no one had been to see Lady Mary in almost a year. She sat day after day in her dark castle room with nothing new to think of. She couldn't just come down to the houses now and sit with the other old crones to spin thread. She had lived like a stranger among them for fifteen years, and it was too late to do anything about it.

Maddie walked back from the castle, thinking sad thoughts. She spied the wood-carver sitting on his favorite boulder, his head bent over a small figure that he was shaping with a knife. Maddie walked up quietly, remembering the day a few weeks ago when he had sat on that same rock and she had pointed out the hills to him. Then he hadn't spoken a word to her. Now he spoke to her all the time, although he rarely spoke to the others.

She stopped, as she had before, to watch him turn the carving. He was so clever, so much more interesting than everyone else. His shadow stretched out before him, long and faint. She remembered her dream about the shadow that hissed, and smiled to herself.

But his shadow was darker, surely, than her own shadow beside it. Maddie blinked and looked again. Darker still, changing color by the minute, like night falling over the world. It lay on the ground, dense and black, wavering and feeling about. Then, like a man crawling on his elbows, it began to move toward her.

"Hey!" cried Maddie. Caught unaware, the carver jumped, and knife and wood went flying. He spun, leaping from the rock like a man facing attack. Then he saw who was there, and his hostile expression eased.

"What happened?" he demanded.

"Your shadow!" she stammered, pointing to the ground behind him. "It moved! Moved by itself. I saw it."

He turned to look, and she looked, too. His shadow was exactly like hers, long and thin and gray in the overcast evening. Maddie blushed hotly, waiting for him to laugh at her.

But the young man didn't laugh. He just watched his shadow for a minute. When he straightened up and faced her again, his green eyes were wary.

"Are you going to tell the others?" he wanted to know.

Maddie's blush deepened. "They'd think I was daft."

She watched him turn away and hunt for his knife and block of wood. "I had a dream about it," she explained. "Your shadow, I mean. It was black, and it hissed at me, and it killed all the grass it touched."

Carver found his knife and stowed it back in the leather holder. "That's silly, Madeleine," he said. "A shadow can't kill things. It needs flesh and bones for that."

"Oh," said the girl, feeling shaky and thoroughly foolish.

"It can't hurt you," he went on seriously. "It just wants to, that's all. But I won't let it. You know that, don't you? You know I wouldn't let anything happen to you."

Maddie stopped feeling foolish. She felt her skin crawl. She stared at the long, harmless shadow on the grass and the strange young man who cast it.

"Don't tell the others," repeated the carver. Maddie managed a smile. He was so handsome and clever, and he cared for her. He wanted her to be safe and well.

"I won't," she promised. "They'd laugh at me." But she knew in her heart that they wouldn't.

# 6

By day, Ned puffed along behind Mad Angus, herding the cattle, and he was locked up with the giant in his stall at night. The old Traveler was the only one who minded. Maddie was delighted with the arrangement. She spent her free time with the mysterious wood-carver, and she grew fonder and fonder of him, in part because he was so obviously attached to her. She was still the only person to whom he spoke freely, the only one in whom he confided his troubles. He was almost well now, and her neighbors respected the quick work he made of their broken tools. Maddie put the hissing shadow from her mind. She began to daydream of a future in which the good-looking carver boy stayed by her hearth.

Then tragedy jarred the town. Bess's mother went into labor, and when the child was born, the women scattered, wailing. The baby had the face of an animal, they said. It had the mouth of a beast.

The townspeople gathered outside the smith's house, whispering together. Maddie stood with them, her arm around Bess, and her frightened cousins gathered near her. Their father was away from home, doing work for the new lord. The smith often traveled from town to town.

"This is evil work," said Little Ian. "The mother was bewitched."

"It's unnatural," agreed Black Ewan, "like that attack on the wood-carver."

"The babe won't live through the day," Old Peggy announced from the door. A grandmother herself, she was the town's midwife. "He's a weak little thing, and his mouth isn't made right. He can't nurse."

"We'll have the baptism right away," rumbled Father Mac, coming out, too. "He has just as much right to heaven as any other little child." The priest hurried off to the church to gather the things he needed.

A wave of relief ran through the crowd. These were normal events. Many babies died soon after birth. Four of this newborn's brothers and sisters already lay in the churchyard. It was good that such an unnatural child would soon be at peace, but that didn't change the horror of what had happened.

"There's someone working evil among us," declared Black Ewan, heading back to the fields. He spat. "God's curse on that black soul."

"Aye, he's right," sighed Old Peggy. "That poor murdered baby. Come with me, lambs," she said to the smith's children. "I've a bit of honeycomb for you. Little ones can't understand these things, and that's all to the good." She and Bess herded them away.

The crowd broke up, heads down and hearts heavy. Maddie picked up her egg basket and started off, but Carver seized her hand. "Wait, Madeleine," he whispered.

Maddie stayed behind as her neighbors walked away, trying to reason with herself. She was absurdly pleased to have her hand held, but she could tell the young man didn't mean anything by it. He was turning her hand nervously between his long fingers as if it were a block of wood he was carving.

"Do you think that's true?" he asked when they were alone. "That something evil harmed that baby before he could be born?"

"They say witches can steal milk without leaving their homes," she replied. "If a witch can take the milk that's inside a cow, it could change a baby inside its mother. Who do you think it could be?"

"I don't know any witches," he muttered, "but I know other evil things." Maddie couldn't help glancing at his shadow as he spoke. He followed her gaze and realized that he still held her hand. He immediately dropped it.

"I need to talk to Black Ewan," he decided. "I need him to let Ned go. It's time for us to leave."

"To leave!" she exclaimed, dismayed. "You don't need to leave."

"I can't stay," he muttered, staring at the ground. "There's harm being done. He has to release Ned. I've mended enough of his tools now, he owes me that."

So that was why he was working on the farm tools, thought Maddie. She had hoped he was settling into their life, but he was just trying to escape.

Carver didn't get a chance to talk to the farmer. Maddie's uncle Colin the Smith returned from his journey, walking back through the grain fields. Unaware of the tragedy surrounding his dying son, the smith nevertheless had information of his own.

"The new lord's wife is dead," he told those he met, and the men left their tools in the fields and gathered around. The women didn't go to funerals, not even for one of their own, but if the men weren't there to help bear the lady's body, they would earn the new lord's lasting fury.

"We'll set out at once," declared Black Ewan. "But without you, Colin. Your family needs you. James, Gillies, and Thomas, you come. Little Ian and Horse, you stay with Colin and finish what you can of the harvest. Don't cut any more grain till you've stored what we've already cut. And, Horse, look after the red mare's injured flank."

"But the storms!" objected Horse. "The harvest will take too long." The least gifted of Black Ewan's farmhands, he was called Horse because he had once lost the one he was riding home during a drunken stupor.

"No storms are here yet," replied Black Ewan. "And we'd best hope we're back before they are." He turned to his nephew. "Lachlan, take care of your mother and keep an eye on the town. Don't try to chain Angus and that Englishman up to the stable wall while I'm gone. Just leave them chained together. Angus won't go anywhere at night with that dead weight to lug around."

Lachlan was only twelve, and he still looked like a child. "Yes, Uncle," he said respectfully. "But hadn't I better keep the key in case something goes wrong?"

Black Ewan looked down at the boy, hesitating. "All right," he answered, pulling the key from his neck and handing it to Lachlan. The boy hung the large key around his own neck, his eyes shining with pride.

"You see?" he boasted to his prisoners that night as the pair lay sprawled in the hay of the stall. "I'm the one who has your key now." But before another day passed, he had reason to regret it.

"Lachlan won't let Ned go," worried Carver the next morning as he and Maddie stacked peats by the houses. He was so distracted that he was more of a hindrance than a help. He stacked one block, walked away, and then came back to stack another. "He has to let him go, he has to," he said, taking down the part she had just finished and restacking it himself. "I don't know what to do."

"Did you think he would?" Maddie asked, taking advantage of his walking away again to fix the mess he was making of the stack. "Lachlan knows good and well that his uncle will thrash him if he lets Ned loose."

"No, he said he wasn't afraid of a beating," contradicted the wood-carver, coming back to dismantle the peats again. Maddie stood up and watched him with a sigh. "He has to let Ned go. Just for a couple of days. Ned will be back before Black Ewan comes home."

"Do you think Lachlan would believe that?" she asked.

"Believe what?" demanded Carver, standing up to look at her, surrounded by mounds of peats. "Madeleine, please," he begged, his eyes very tired. "Just for a couple of days."

The girl frowned and stepped up close to lay her hand on his cheek. "Your fever's back," she announced. "I might have known. It's back, and it's high."

"I know that," he muttered. "No, wait—" But she was already calling her mother.

"I never should have let him do all that work!" exclaimed Fair Sarah, and she soon had the young man under piles of blankets again, ignoring his protests. "I'd better stay with him," she told Maddie. "He might wander off in this state, and he'll not listen to you. Bring me the baskets and shuttles, and I'll wind yarn for your father till he sleeps."

But Carver wasn't the only one bent on obtaining the Traveler's release. Ned was brooding in the cow pasture, fingering the padlock at his ankle. Lachlan came past, heading toward the workers singing in the grain fields, and he grinned at the sight.

"Stick your thumb in the keyhole and turn it to the left," he jeered. Ned looked up quickly.

"Lachlan, golden-haired boy," he wheedled. "Pity on an old man, and let me out. I'll give my blessing on you."

The boy came over to stand before his prisoners. Mad Angus was gazing blankly up at the clouds, but the Englishman's faded eyes were fixed on him. "Your blessing!" He laughed. "A drunkard's blessing. What good's that?"

"It's you I think of," whined the Traveler. "Take pity."

Lachlan's eyes were bright, and he looked at his prized key thoughtfully. "Beg me," he proposed. "On your knees."

The old man rolled onto his knees. "I do beg. Use the key."

The boy stood over him, chest puffed out, glorying in the moment. "No," he said at last. He made a rude face and turned away.

Ned seized a large branch that he had found in his trips around the pastures and gave the boy a sharp blow to the side of the head. He chuckled as Lachlan slid into a heap at his feet, and he jerked the key from the boy's neck.

"I use the key, then," he told the huddled form, "and I keep my blessing."

But just as Ned bent to unlock the padlock, Mad Angus spotted a calf that needed chasing, and he was off with a bellow. Ned hopped after him, cursing, the key swinging uselessly from his hands. Then Horse came over the turf dyke and spotted his master's injured boy. He charged at the old man, fists flying, and soon another body lay still on the ground.

Horse retrieved the key, spat on that greasy gray

hair, and carried Lachlan off toward the houses. Mad Angus stood in confusion for a minute, tugging on the chain and looking down at the crumpled form. Then he picked up the Traveler's limp body and slung it over his shoulder. Problem solved, he took off after the cows again.

All the women who weren't in the fields came running when Horse brought in Lachlan. His mother had him laid in the box bed, and Father Mac studied the mark of the cudgel.

"Pour wine into the wound," he suggested and fetched some of his own stock for the purpose. They burned feathers under the boy's nose, but Lachlan wouldn't wake up.

"Maddie, run for Lady Mary," said Fair Sarah, and Maddie hurried off to the gray castle. There sat the old woman with last year's embroidery work, pulling out the fragile threads for her new design because she had run out of colors.

"I found a mistake in this," she lied, and she hastily rolled up the canvas. Maddie realized with a shock that now no one would send her more thread. No one would pay her more visits.

"There's news," she said guiltily, watching the proud woman.

"I don't want to hear it," sniffed Lady Mary.

"The new lord's wife is dead. The men left to bear the body."

Lady Mary sat for a little while without moving. Then she set aside the roll of cloth and climbed to her feet.

"Is that what you came to say?" she demanded, walking over to stare out her little window. "You hurried up here to tell me, didn't you? Bad news can't wait."

Maddie remembered her errand. She explained about the Traveler's hitting Lachlan and stealing the key, and she told how Horse had discovered the theft in progress and brought the unconscious boy home.

"So he thought one good blow was enough to set him free," muttered the old woman. "It takes more than that."

"Please, do you come," urged Maddie. "Lachlan won't wake up, and his mother's anxious."

"I'll not set foot in that house!" declared Lady Mary angrily. "Do you think I don't know what Black Ewan says about me? Do you think I don't know what they all say?" She turned from the window, her face fallen into seams and wrinkles, and her eyes were sick with despair. "You all think it, I know," she challenged. "Every last one of you."

"I'm sorry," said Maddie, and she meant it. There was something terribly pitiful about the lonely, rich old woman.

"Ah, you're a good girl," sighed Lady Mary, going back to her chair. She sat down and bowed her head. "Tell them to leave him quiet, and he'll likely wake up in the end. There's nothing I can do for a rapped skull."

Maddie delivered her message to the assembly of women and went to her own house. Carver was lying there staring up through the hazy smoke and picking dead grass stems from the wall.

"What's happened now?" he whispered. "Your mother left, and I can hear everyone coming and going."

Maddie sat down by him on her mother's stool and began winding the abandoned yarn. "It's your old Ned that's done it this time," she said. "He's likely killed a boy." She told him about the theft. He listened without speaking, his eyes bright with the fever and his fingers turning and fidgeting as if they held his carving tools.

"Madeleine, go talk to Ned for me," he said at last. "Go ask him what I'm supposed to do."

"That criminal? Why do you need his advice? What do you mean, what you're supposed to do?"

"He'll know," he whispered. "Promise me you'll do it." So Maddie sighed and went.

She made her way out to the cow pasture to the two companions in chains. They were looking more and more like they belonged together. With his new black eye and the blood crusted in the stubbly growth of his beard, the Englishman looked simply ghastly.

"You've likely murdered Lachlan," she informed him in answer to his cheerful greeting.

"Ah, he ain't dead," grunted the battered old man peaceably. "That brat needed learning."

"Carver sent me," she explained. "He says you have to tell him what to do. He wants to leave, but his fever's back, so I say you should tell him to rest for a while."

Ned swatted the midges away from his bruised face and gazed thoughtfully up at the sky. "You're fond of him," he considered. "In love of him. The lad's caught your fancy."

"He has," admitted the forthright Maddie, who saw no reason to lie.

"But what sort are you?" he asked, fixing her with a surprisingly keen stare. "Some featherbrain chick with no guts? Faint and scream and run to her folks with every little trouble?"

"I am not," declared Maddie firmly. "I can face my share of trouble."

"More than your share?" he demanded. "Can you keep your head in bad times? Can you keep a secret?"

"He's in trouble, isn't he?" breathed the girl. "I knew it! I'll help, and I won't ever tell."

"You'd be just the one," muttered the Traveler with a bloody, pink-toothed grin. "I can see that clear enough. You think you're the one he needs— oh, yes, you're better for him than I be. Swear on your soul you won't give him over. Swear to stand by him if I tell."

"I swear," said Maddie, and she made the sign of the cross. "May I lose heaven if I fail."

"You'll lose more than that," muttered Ned. "You do just what I say, just like I say, or you'll be dead in two days. And if you tell the secret to any-one, your lad will be dead in that same hour."

# 7

Maddie made her way back to the house and gave Carver his instructions.

"You!" gasped the young man, sitting up. "Madeleine, not you!"

"Yes, me," affirmed Maddie. "There's no one else you can trust."

"But I didn't want it to be you!" he cried, looking wild.

"Well, it is," she replied sensibly. "The Englishman told me what to do, and it doesn't sound very hard. He says you're to leave today so no one will suspect. I'll leave before sundown tomorrow evening, and you can meet me at the rotten stump that's just out of sight of the castle. Go now, while Ma's out, or you won't have another chance till night."

She took down some dried fish for him and cut out a firm square of the morning's cold porridge. He pushed off the blankets and climbed to his feet, watching her work.

"And you'll be there well before dark," he cautioned. "Twilight is too late."

"I know all about it," she replied with confidence. He hesitated, eyeing her doubtfully. "Be off, then," she said, handing him the food.

Fair Sarah was very upset when she returned and found her sick boy gone. "The night is cold," she worried to Maddie. "He'll take a bad turn, just like Angus did. I never should have left him. It's little enough I could do to help. Lachlan hasn't stirred."

Maddie rehearsed her speech the next day as she went about her work. At noon, she took food to her mother and the other women working in the fields.

"Lady Mary is upset about the death of the new lord's wife," she said, sitting by her mother as she ate. "She told me at breakfast she wants me to stay with her in the castle tonight."

"Poor woman," sighed Fair Sarah. "Do that for her, Maddie. It's a work of mercy, I'd say." And the girl walked off, consumed with guilt. She had never lied to her mother before.

Late that afternoon, Maddie took supper to Lady Mary and paused, looking out the castle doorway. No one was nearby. They were in the fields or at Black Ewan's house, sitting with Lachlan's mother over her unconscious child. Maddie took the path beside the loch that led away from the castle and the houses.

The wood-carver emerged from the forest by the rotten stump, and they walked down the path together. Maddie told him the news about Lachlan and the work in the fields, but he didn't make any comment. The fever seemed to be working on him. His face was deadly pale. The loch sparkled, and the pine trees were dark green, shading the path now and again with their thick boughs. But the sun already sat on the rim of the high, bare hills across the water.

"This is the Place of the Hands," noted Maddie as the path crossed marshy land beside the loch. "It used to be that folk who walked through this place at dusk would see hands carrying a light down the path before them. Then, in Old Dad's time, the pig-man and his wife were cutting their peats in the bog yonder, and they found a pair of severed hands in the peat, still roped together. They brought them back and buried them in the churchyard under a stone that just says 'Hands,' and no one ever saw the light on the path again."

"We need to hurry," muttered the young man, glancing at the sinking sun.

In another few minutes, Carver left the path and walked a few feet into the bracken, approaching the rocky face of the steep hill that climbed into the sky beside them. Maddie followed him to a narrow crack in the rock wall, just wide enough for a man to slip through. He knelt to retrieve a lighted lantern from the shelter of the narrow cave. Holes pierced in the metal sides let in air, and one side was covered by a thin panel of horn. The light shone through it and into the crack in the cliff, illuminating it with a dusky tan glow.

"I know this place," announced Maddie with satisfaction. "It's the Cave of the Arrows. Look, someone's made the opening bigger."

She ran her finger along one edge of the crack. Large chunks and flakes of rock had been chiseled from its sides and littered the ground at their feet. The young man stopped to look at them, picking up a big fragment. Then he tossed it aside.

"There's no time," he said and stepped into the narrow opening, holding up the light. The pierced sides of the lantern made crazy patterns on the rough, seamed rock as they hurried along, climbing over fallen boulders and avoiding the mossy faces of wet walls.

"First to the right and then to the left," he said as they turned down a side passage. A couple of hundred feet beyond the second turning, their tunnel widened and made a sharp bend. Someone had driven an iron ring into the wall at that bend and attached to it a stout length of chain.

Carver set the lantern down at the beginning of the rough room. He walked to the chain and lifted it to reveal an iron collar at its free end. He fastened the large, unwieldy collar loosely around his neck, sliding a metal guard over the catch. Maddie watched him with interest, standing by the lantern.

"You know what to do," he reminded her.

"I stay here in plain sight where the cave widens," she recited. "I distract you until you change, and then I can leave."

"Be sure you don't come any closer," he cautioned. "Stay away from me. I can come to here." He stopped about ten feet from her. He began pacing at the end of the chain as she watched from the passageway. "I wish it weren't you, Madeleine," he said. "I wish it were someone else."

"Does it hurt?" asked Maddie.

"I don't know," he answered, walking back and forth in an arc. "I can't remember anything about it. Except it's like a nightmare, like waking up after a bad dream."

"Why do you need to be distracted?" she asked. He kept walking, staring at the ground.

"Once I'm changed, my hands are too clumsy to work the buckle. But if I don't have anything to think about before I'm changed all the way, I can still unfasten the collar," he said. "If someone's here, I don't think to do that."

"Why don't you just use a padlock?" the practical Maddie wanted to know.

"And do what with the key?" he asked impatiently. "If it's within reach, I might throw it away somewhere during the night, and if you take it, you might trip over a root and break your neck out there. Either way, I starve to death chained to this wall.

Even if you come back without the key, I'm dead. You couldn't get this collar off without it, and no blacksmith will let me go. He'll find out why I'm like this and then kill me."

Maddie thought about that for a minute. "What do you change into?" she asked.

"Don't you know?" countered the young man, stopping to stare at her. "Didn't Ned tell you what happens?"

"Not anything that made sense," she replied.

"You have to not run away," he said urgently. "Not till I'm completely changed, no matter what. I'll come after you. I'll kill you if you run away too soon."

"I won't," she answered defensively. He continued to stare at her.

"Come here," he said. And Maddie almost went. She took a step, then paused.

"Why?" she wanted to know.

"Because I *told* you to, you stinking brat!"

Maddie looked at the young man in astonishment. He began pacing rapidly to and fro as close as he could come to her, staring at her all the while.

"You smell," he said, his eyes glittering with excitement. "You smell like sweat. You smell like blood. You spineless slug, you mound of mud, come *here!*" he shrieked. "Just three more steps, and wouldn't *you* get a surprise!"

Maddie blinked. A black shadow seemed to lie across his face. His eyes gleamed out through it, brilliantly green. She stooped and lifted the lantern to shine it full on him, but the shadow on his face didn't move.

"You blister," he snarled, his voice harsh and rough. "You squashy bubble of blood. Just one little *tug,* and the bones come all apart. Just one little *prick,* and it all comes gushing out!"

Shadow lay around him, spreading out and climbing up the cave walls. Those eyes were like lamps above her now, round and glowing.

"*Blood,*" purred the shadow in a thick voice. "*Salty, sweaty blood.*"

The black figure was indistinct in the dimness of the cave, flickering in the darkness. Maddie couldn't see anymore where it began and where it ended. It seemed to reach out and engulf her little pool of lantern light. It swung its arms, and she heard a metal clashing, like big knives being sharpened.

"*Come here now!*" it screamed. It bent over her in the darkness, and the lantern flickered and dimmed.

*"I'm hungry!"* wailed the shadow in an agony of greed. *"Warm blood! I'm hungry!"*

Gripping the lantern, Maddie tore off down the passage, the light forming wild patterns on the walls. She tripped over a boulder, and the candle flame guttered and sank almost to nothing. The darkness pressed in around her.

*"Come back!"* sobbed that thick voice, echoing along the passage. *"Come back so I can eat you alive!"*

# 8

The opening of the cave was in sight before her, a narrow rectangle of cool gray twilight. Maddie dropped the lantern and scrambled out into the semidarkness. She ran until she thought her lungs would burst. Her sides ached as she stumbled along, the loch waters rustling beside her and the steep folds of the hills shadowing her way. On and on she ran until the hard, square bulk of the castle stood before her and the black mouth of its open doorway welcomed her in. She careered headlong up the stone steps in the darkness and flung herself into the friendly candlelight of Lady Mary's hall.

Lady Mary was sitting up in bed, her long white hair in a braid and the curtain by her head pulled back so she could read in the light of the candle. She gaped in astonishment at the girl who stood gasping on the landing, unable to speak.

The old woman hurried over and steered her toward the light. Maddie collapsed onto a padded bench, her whole body sore. A minute later, a silver cup appeared beside her, and Lady Mary sat down on the bed.

"What happened? Is it Black Ewan's boy?" she asked, looking very worried.

Maddie took ragged breaths and listened to the pounding of her heart. She thought about the wood-carver and her happy daydreams. Then she relived for just an instant what had happened in the cave, and her daydreams crumbled into revulsion. But she mustn't give anything away. She had sworn on her soul. She had made a promise to protect him, no matter what he was, and she was determined to keep it.

"I brought your food," she gasped, "and I went down the path by the loch. I saw a thing, and I followed it. But when night fell, it put me in mind of that thing that attacked the carver. I came running back, thinking it was chasing me."

Lady Mary walked to the window. "What did your thing look like?" she asked, a hint of amusement in her voice.

"It looked like a shadow," answered the girl. "A big black shadow."

"Maybe you saw a werewolf," suggested the old woman, looking out the window. "Tonight is the full moon."

Maddie sat still in shock. A werewolf! An evil creature that changed with the moon. When had she faced that hissing shape in the doorway? Was it a month ago that she had dreamed of her town littered with bones?

"But it didn't look like a wolf," she whispered.

"I don't think they do," replied Lady Mary, turning from the window. "People call them wolves because of their connection to the moon. I have a book about them around here somewhere, but I haven't looked at it in a long time. You'd best be home, girl. Your mother will worry."

"I don't want to go back out there," answered Maddie, and that at least was the perfect truth.

"Couldn't I just stay on this bench? I won't make a sound."

"Come up into bed by me," proposed the old woman. "That's where Kathleen used to sleep before she died and quit my service. I do miss that girl."

Maddie scrambled into the soft bed with Lady Mary and pulled the linen sheets up to her nose. Kathleen was Black Ewan's childhood sweetheart. He missed her, too, said all the town widows. It was strange, reflected the tired girl, that the love of the same person could turn two people to hatred.

The next morning, Maddie was up in the gray dawn to go to Mass. Lachlan's mother was there, too, her face like a light. Her boy had woken up at last. He didn't remember anything about what had happened the last two days, but he had eaten all the food she cooked him and begged for more.

How fervent Maddie was in Mass that morning! God had spared her to look on another day. Safe in the damp little church, she thought about the evil shadow in the cave. Thank God it hadn't gotten her. Pray God it never would.

Ned spotted her as she gathered eggs. "You're alive," he called cheerfully.

"I did just what you told me to do," she said with a shudder, coming over to him. Mad Angus was dozing out of the wind. She looked around and lowered her voice. "Is he a werewolf?" she asked.

"He is," confirmed the Englishman. "Ugly brute, ain't he? Ain't a ugly enough name."

"Was he the same thing that came to my house?" she wanted to know. The old man nodded.

"That was a long night," he said. "I was afraid. Up all night. At last I decided he can't get out of the cave. That's when I heard him scream." Maddie thought of the stone shards at the cave mouth. That's what had made the crack wider.

"But how is it possible?" she demanded. "That creature tore up Carver. It couldn't have been him."

"It was him," affirmed the Traveler calmly. "The farmhands say you hit him with something. You cut him, I think. When he smelled the blood, he can't stand it. Then he cut himself."

The weather was gray and dreary, with a chilly wind. The men were still away from home. Maddie thought about the wood-carver all day long without meaning to think of him at all. Part of her was waiting for him to come back, and part of her was dreading it. She didn't think she wanted to see him again.

"I wonder where my poor, sick boy is," sighed Fair Sarah as they ate their lonely meal. "I hope he's warm. It's good we got the grain stacked. There's rain coming in from the west."

Fair Sarah's sick boy didn't come back all day, and Maddie couldn't help wondering why. Maybe he had strangled on that chain, or maybe he had wandered away into the tunnels of the cave. Maybe he never meant to come back. Maybe he was ashamed to, now that she knew.

Maddie thought about that, about how upset he had been that she would be there. Of course he must be ashamed. He hadn't wanted her to see him. She remembered his handsome face and wary eyes, his low voice talking to her. He wasn't the son of a chief, and he wasn't perfect, either, but she had admitted that she loved him, and she had promised to protect him. She should find out what was wrong.

After she took Lady Mary the evening meal, she made the walk down the path again. The cold air had settled to the bottom of the valley, and the wind whipped across the steel-gray water. It was growing dark when she reached the cave. She knelt in the entrance to light the lantern with the chunk of burning peat she had brought and crept cautiously down the narrow tunnel, her heart stopping at every shadow.

A body slumped on the ground at the end of the iron chain, indistinct in the feeble light. Setting down the lantern, she inched fearfully toward the silent figure. She found no snarling, bubbling monster. The wood-carver lay shivering in the grip of a high fever. His lean face looked frail and pinched, and when she touched him, he moaned in pain.

There's no sense just standing here, thought the practical girl, and she set to work. She managed to unfasten the heavy collar and lift it from his neck, but he was unconscious, and no efforts roused him. She dragged him across the room before she realized that she would never get him home. Tucking his sheepskin blanket around him, Maddie puzzled over the problem of moving him out of the cave, but she could think of no solution. She hurried away into the cloudy night.

The next morning, she was out of the house before dawn and down the path again. Her mother was gullible enough to think she was at morning Mass because Maddie had never deceived her before, but someone else was bound to notice her trips back and forth if she didn't get him home soon.

The wood-carver still jerked and cried out in delirium, but she managed to get him onto his knees and staggering a short distance. Time after time, she urged him up and helped him crawl a little, his progress lit by the lantern on the ground in front of them. At last she got him out of the cave and into the cold shadows of morning as a thin rain began to drizzle down. But the path was too long, and he was desperately ill. Maddie wrapped the sheepskin around his hot, shivering form, and then she tucked her own checked blanket around him, watching the tiny drops of rain trickle down his black hair. She hurried up the path again, thinking about what to do.

"Father Mac," she called as the priest left the little stone church.

"Where were you, child?" he boomed. "You weren't in Mass."

"No, I've found something, Father, and I'm needing your help." She led the priest down the path by the loch.

"What were you doing here so early?" he wondered, squinting into the rain.

"Looking," answered Maddie, thinking furiously. "I hoped Carver might be coming home, and then I found him."

Father Mac knelt down by the delirious wood-carver, eyeing the chipped and widened cave entrance with a puzzled frown. Then he picked the young man up with a grunt and heaved him across his shoulder.

Fair Sarah was beside herself with anxiety and relief when her sick boy came home. "I knew he was wandering like Angus!" she exclaimed, stripping the wet shirt from him. "He'll kill himself yet with this cold and damp. He's raving again, just raving!"

Maddie huddled by the peat fire to warm herself and watched her mother fuss over Carver. She sat next to the fire and teased baskets of loose wool that day, combing out the brambles while he groaned and whispered. It was just like it had been a month ago, but now everything was different. Before, she had been fascinated by the mysterious young man. Now she knew the mystery.

Next morning, the wood-carver still shivered and shook, but he was back in his right mind. He waited until Fair Sarah went out into the dripping rain, and then he called to Maddie.

"What did I do?" he asked her, just as he had before. She stared at him, thinking about what he had done. The insults. The hatred. The horror.

"Nothing," she said shortly. Then she realized she should say more. "I did what I was supposed to," she elaborated, "and when you didn't come back, I went and fetched you. Father Mac carried you home partway, but nobody knows except me."

"So I didn't do anything? Nothing at all?" he asked, watching her guarded expression. Maddie shook her head. She was telling a lie, and they both knew it. She had told more lies in the last three days than in the three years before them.

The wood-carver stared at the cobwebbed ceiling with hollow eyes, and Maddie turned to leave. "Wait," he whispered. "Just a little longer." She sat down on her mother's stool and waited.

"I had a name," he began quietly. "My name used to be Paul. I was a MacLean, from the Island of Trees. Our house stood by a little mill over the water, away from all the other houses. My father was a wood-carver, his father, too, and he taught me and my older brother. I used to follow the cows and stay with them days while I did a bit of carving.

"One night something happened. Something

terrible happened. I woke up, and my sisters were screaming, my mother, too, and I heard my father shouting. I wasn't very old, only seven or eight, and I didn't go out to help. I crawled under the box bed, curled up as small as I could. Then no more shouts, just screams, even from my father and my brother. Ripping and crashing and other sounds— I can't even think about them. Another scream, loud and long, a scream right out of hell. And then silence, except for breathing. My breathing, and something else breathing. And then something in the room began to talk."

The wood-carver turned on his pillow, cringing at the memory, and his anxious eyes found her face. "It was talking to me," he said, almost in a whisper. "It knew where I was hiding. It said—but I can't tell you what it said. I can't ever tell you what it said. It dragged me out from under the bed, and I don't know what it looked like, but it was big, bigger than a man, with big round eyes. It bit me on the shoulder with huge teeth, bit me so deep I thought it would bite me in half.

"I don't know what happened then. Maybe I fainted. But the next thing I knew, it was morning, and light was coming in through the door. I was lying in a puddle of blood. Not a puddle—a lake of blood. The room around me was torn apart. And my family—they were torn apart, too. Blood splashed up the walls and onto the blankets, it was just like slaughtering day. And next to me was a man I'd never seen, lying there sound asleep. When I moved, he woke and sat up, and his face was covered with blood. He looked at me, all confused, and then he burst into tears. He sobbed out loud like a baby, running his bloody hands through his hair.

"Then Ned came running in, puffing—I'd never seen him before that day. But he burst into tears, too, and he and that man cried and cried, but me, I don't think I cried at all. They took my shirt off to look at the bite, it was like the teeth of a trap had dug into me. Then Ned found our big butchering knife and gave it to the man, and he crawled off behind the oatmeal chest, and I didn't see him again. Ned caught me by the arms and helped me out into the yard. He told me we were leaving, so I took my father's carving tools from his bench by the door. Ned set the house on fire, and we walked away and left it, and I've never been back there again."

The carver took a deep breath and passed his hands over his face. Then he composed himself again, looking away from her.

"Ned has places all over the country, hiding places for me when I change. We never stay anywhere very long so no one takes notice of us. Ned told me that day that I don't have a name anymore because I'm dead just like my folks. The bite took my life away even though I seem alive. He said I have to stay away from the living because I can't ever live again. My kind kills people that we love."

Maddie stared at that white face, too shocked to speak. She thought of the little boy left alive in a pool of his own parents' blood.

"I didn't want you to know," he whispered. "Not you, most of all. I'm something horrible, Madeleine. I don't mean to be. I know what you think of me now."

Maddie felt tears come to her eyes. But it was silly to cry, she told herself firmly. This was something crying wouldn't mend.

"No, I don't think that," she answered slowly. "I'm not sorry I know, Paul." She slipped out of the house and left him alone, still staring up at the ceiling.

# 9

All that rainy day, Maddie and her cousins sat on the floor of her uncle's empty forge and peeled rushes while the short black chickens scratched through the peelings and clucked over small bugs. It took a knack to strip the fibers from the pulp so that it would give a good light when soaked in fat, but even the little children knew how to do it. Soon they would need these lights. Darkness was coming, the time of year when the days were short and stormy. Maddie felt that those dark days were already here.

As she sat there, working mindlessly, absorbed in horrifying thoughts, a voice in her head kept laughing at her. *You wanted to know all about him,* it taunted. He was so exciting and mysterious. Well, now you know the mystery, don't you, you and your stupid curiosity.

You're in trouble, she told herself fiercely as she split and peeled the rushes. This is real trouble, big trouble, and it's bigger than you are. It belongs to big, worldly men like Father Mac and Black Ewan. But as she worked, she imagined what the men would do about it. It was just like the old Traveler had told her. Paul would be dead that same hour.

"I'll bet you're glad the wood-carver's back," remarked Bess as she shooed away a chicken.

"Why?" asked Maddie absently.

"You know why," prompted Bess with a grin, but Maddie shook her head.

That evening, Maddie swept Lady Mary's dusty corner as the old woman ate fish soup.

"If a werewolf's not a wolf, what is it?" she wanted to know.

"Why do you ask a question like that?" demanded Lady Mary.

"Because of your book about them," answered the girl. "Who can tell, I might meet up with one."

Lady Mary finished her supper. "I doubt it," she

remarked, "if you stop chasing shadows. I was just rereading that book, as a matter of fact."

She picked up a small volume from one of the stacks and handed it to Maddie, watching the girl turn the brown vellum pages and run her finger over the black strokes of the crowded letters. "I should have taught you to read Latin," she sighed.

Maddie looked up from the puzzling page. "Bless you!" she laughed. "As if I could read anything!" She handed back the book.

"But no one else asks the questions you ask," observed Lady Mary. "You'd like to read, I think. What is a werewolf? It's closer to being a flea or a louse than a wolf. Fleas, lice, and werewolves are all parasites. They live on a host. A werewolf is a spirit or being of some kind that lives with a person. On the night of the full moon, it takes over entirely, making the person do what it wants. It's related to the undead. It may even be the same type of parasite, except that the undead inhabits a corpse."

"But if it's there all the time, why doesn't it always make the person do what it wants?"

"The undead seems to do that," admitted Lady Mary. "It walks whenever it pleases at night. But the werewolf inhabits a living human, and the human has to stay living. If a werewolf were a werewolf every night, how long would its person survive? A few nights, maybe. Then it would die of exhaustion or be caught and killed, and with its host dead, the werewolf inside it is dead, too. Unless it becomes one of the undead. My book isn't sure."

Maddie thought about Paul in his fever, half delirious even now. He must be sick around every full moon. That deathly pale face, those long white fingers. A poison was drying up his blood. He couldn't survive it night after night. It would be too much for him.

"How does a person become a werewolf?" she asked. Lady Mary was reading her book.

"Oh, it's classic," she replied absently. "It comes from a bite, just like the mad dog's bite that makes others go mad. It's like a very strange illness."

"Then what's the cure?" demanded Maddie.

"The cure?" murmured the old woman. "A werewolf is killed, and his body is burned, just like a mad dog. Or the werewolf is burned from the start, burned to death, taking care of both requirements at once."

"But that's no cure!" gasped Maddie in horror.

"It's a good idea. It prevents new victims from becoming werewolves—assuming the poor burned fools were werewolves to start with."

"So there's no way to heal a werewolf," concluded the girl bitterly.

"I honestly don't know if the book tells," answered Lady Mary. "I'm still rereading it. I don't see why you'd be so upset about it," she added with a smile.

Maddie felt numb and miserable. "Why wouldn't I be upset to know that some people find out burning to death is their only cure?"

Lady Mary's smile slipped, and a shadow appeared in her eyes. Maddie felt cold at the sight of it. "I know just how you feel," whispered the proud old woman. "You'd better be going now."

Maddie came home through the dim, wet twilight to find Paul asleep. She stood by the settle to look at him. Bone-white and thin. Sick with an illness that had murder as its goal and burning as its only cure.

She heard Black Ewan's dogs barking excitedly, and Little Ian's dog joined in. Men's voices hailed each other in the darkness. Her mother jumped to her feet, dropping her knitting, as James Weaver ducked under the doorpost and unwrapped his wet blanket from his shoulders.

"Ah, wife," he said, kissing her, "have you any food for a hungry man?" He spotted the sleeping Carver. "What ails the lad now?"

"His fever's back," replied Fair Sarah, taking eggs from the basket and meal from the chest. "He wandered for two days out of his mind before Father Mac found him by the loch. It's a mysterious illness. The boy never seems to grow stronger."

The next morning was Sunday, and the towns-people were all in Mass together. Father Mac reminded them of the reasons they had to thank God. The grain was out of the fields, the men were home safe, and Lachlan was well again. But some were bent on other business that morning. They had no time to waste on thankfulness.

Carrying her basket to Lady Mary after Mass, Maddie walked by a knot of bystanders. Black Ewan was among them.

"Maddie, come here," he called. "You'll not take another bite to that fiend yonder. If she wants her food, she can come out and face us."

The girl hesitated. Black Ewan had been telling her what to do her whole life. He was the one who made sure that everyone worked and everyone received a share.

"She'll be waiting for her breakfast, surely," she pointed out. "It's late already." But the farmer took the basket away from her.

"Horse, call the others," he ordered. "It's time we talked about this, and today's a good day for it. We can use our rest to some purpose."

The people crowded around Black Ewan right where he stood on the open ground at the edge of the bog. The sky was dark and overcast, and the hills on either side kept appearing like black shadows through the silver bands of clouds. Gulls screamed and wheeled in the sky above them, fishing the choppy waters of the loch.

"I've spoken my mind to the new lord about Lady Mary," announced Black Ewan. "I've told him I believe that the woman is a witch. He admitted to me that she isn't his kin and that she was only a friend of his late wife. He will hear any charge we bring against her and carry out the proper penalty."

"Which means," translated Father Mac in his booming voice, "that the new lord is tired of keeping her, and now that his wife is dead, he'd rather give this castle and town to one of his strong men. It's wasted on an old woman."

"He says he'll try her fairly," retorted Black Ewan. "What's in his mind is up to him, not us."

"He'll try her with fire and torture," countered the priest. "He'll wring a confession from her one way or another. It's up to this town not to bring a false charge against an old woman just because you're tired of feeding her."

"We'd never mind the feeding if she acted like everyone else," protested the farmer. "We feed the widows gladly, and the old ones, too. Old Peggy, and Jeannie Ian, and Tom's Ma, we haven't kept food from you, have we? But Lady Mary's not like the others. And you know she's never in church."

"Just because she doesn't come to church doesn't mean she's a witch," replied the priest. "Lady Mary has odd notions about God, it's true. She comes from the city far away, and all kinds of strange ideas are the fashion there. But I've visited her many times and had talks with her. She's expressed no interest in witchcraft."

"She wouldn't tell you, Father," argued Black Ewan. "It's the fruits that give her away. A bad tree bears bad fruit, and that's what we have from her.

Think back on her time here with us. Many a misfortune has befallen us, and strange things have happened. That creature from the loch tearing up the wood-carver for one thing, and the smith's dead baby for another."

"Are you going to blame every strange thing on her?" demanded Father Mac.

As the debate went on, the mothers began to dispatch children on errands. Supplies arrived, and the women sat down to spin or knit. Colin the Smith brought glowing embers in a pot, and he and Little Ian built a fire. Horse and Gillies added lengths of wood from a rotted tree. The damp splinters steamed and smoked. Soon a bright blaze crackled up.

"There was the time she told me to get my stinking cow out of her way," recalled Little Ian, "and that same cow was struck by lightning within the week."

"And when we went to search the castle when the Water Horse came," remembered Gillies, "she said she'd rather see a Water Horse than us."

"So she's contrary," admitted Father Mac. "But if being contrary meant being a witch, half of us here would be charged and hanged."

Tom's Ma stood up, an ancient, tottering crone.

"'They told me when I was a little girl that a Bible witch talked to dead spirits," she mumbled, her lips sunken around her toothless gums. "This witch does, too. She told me about what some dead Greek said about the spots before my eyes. Now, where's she learning stuff like that if she doesn't talk to spirits?"

"She read it in a book," said Father Mac patiently. "How do you know what King David said, or what St. Paul said? They were dead, too, before you were born."

"I don't know what the good saints have to do with some dead Greek," barked Tom's Ma, and the assembled townspeople murmured together.

"James, you should speak," urged Black Ewan. "Fair Sarah, tell about your daughter's birth."

"I was bad off," said Maddie's mother shortly. "Lady Mary helped me with her potions, and I lived."

"But you never had children after that," observed the farmer. "And who are you to say that it wasn't those potions that took them from you?"

"And who are you to say it was?" demanded Fair Sarah in a temper. She raised her distaff, and Black Ewan took a hasty step back. Every man was afraid of being struck by a woman's distaff. It had magical powers all its own.

The barrage continued throughout the day. Person after person recalled livestock that were cursed, crops that were blighted, and one strange event after another. Maddie stared at the roaring fire and pondered the charges. Lady Mary wasn't like anyone else, and she had no patience with God or her neighbors. But Maddie doubted very much that the old woman would have harmed the smith's unborn child, and she knew the hissing creature that had stood at her door was no Water Horse. She wondered what she should do. She couldn't defend Lady Mary without revealing Paul's secret, and the woodcarver himself wasn't present. The sick young man had wandered over to investigate the assembly, but Fair Sarah had sent him back inside, out of the wind. Maddie could see him appear from time to time in her doorway, too far away to hear.

As the cloudy afternoon wore on, the gathering began to take on an air of unreality. The wood fire blazed with a friendly glow, and the children held wet sticks in it to watch them spark, or hunted for eggs to cook in the hot ashes. Little Ian brought out the last of his stock of the water of life and shared it around as they talked. The voices got louder, and the arguments grew more heated. The stories became wilder.

At last, as the dark day tended toward twilight, out came the witch herself. Lady Mary stomped up the path from the castle in a rage, her fine velvet cloak over her shoulders and a small book in her hand.

"You good-for-nothing!" she cried when she saw Maddie. "Do you think I want to wait all day for my food? I don't care if you idiots want to hold some drunken revel, but you remember your obligations first!"

Black Ewan stepped forward to face her. "You've taken food out of our mouths long enough," he said sternly. "We know you for what you are, you witch, and we're sending you to the new lord to be tried."

"So I'm responsible for all your troubles, I suppose?" scoffed Lady Mary. "Everything from toothache to hangnail. Don't look to me for your evils. You're evil enough by yourselves. I won't stand here arguing with the likes of you. Maddie, bring me my food when they've drunk themselves to sleep." She turned to walk away, but Horse and Gillies blocked her path, and the people crowded around.

"Let's see that book first," proposed Black Ewan. "Let's see what prayer book you were reading on the Lord's Day."

"This book?" Anxiety flickered across the old woman's face. "This is no business of yours."

"We make it our business, witch," said Gillies, and he plucked it from her.

"No!" she cried, trying to grab it back.

"Father, it's in the Pope's tongue," announced Black Ewan, looking at it. "Tell us which of the psalms she was singing."

Father Mac advanced to take the book and turned to the first page.

"'Here begins a treatise on demonical inhabitations,'" he translated, his voice revealing his surprise, "'concerning the possessed man, the malicious lunatic, the werewolf, and the undead.'"

"A spell book! A book of the black arts!" exclaimed the farmer. Father Mac was absorbed in examining the text. He didn't answer the charge.

The whole town was around the old woman now, talking and exclaiming. "Damned witch!"

shouted Little Ian, and someone flung a handful of mud onto her velvet cloak.

"Filthy witch!" cried several voices, and the crowd surged forward.

"Get her to safety, Black Ewan," called Father Mac. "I hold you responsible."

People were shouting and cursing, and Lady Mary was shouting back. Her face was red, and her white hair had come loose from its neat bun and straggled around her face. Black Ewan half-carried, half-dragged her down to the castle, Father Mac's arms around her protectively. Some of the crowd ran to supply themselves with weapons and rocks, but they didn't use them. For the moment, they were unwilling to hit their parish priest.

Father Mac and Black Ewan disappeared into the castle with her. They were intent on the relative safety of the Hole, the simple cell chiseled out of the rock and reached by a trapdoor in the floor of the lowest story. The crowd milled around outside, robbed of its victim. The men had drawn their knives, and women who had patted Maddie's cheek since she was old enough to walk were shrieking out terrible threats.

"Burn her goods!" shrieked Jeannie Ian, and the idea caught on at once.

"Burn out the witch, burn the books of the black arts," echoed a half-dozen voices. Excited boys raced back to the fire by the bog for burning sticks and embers. Townspeople came and went through the castle doorway, bringing her furniture outside. They pulled out the bench, smashed up the table, and threw linen down in a heap on the gravel shore. Maddie saw one of Lady Mary's tapestries and her little embroidered footstool on the pile. Then the fire caught, and the flames went up with a hungry roar.

Maddie raced up the stairs and into the hall. The small brown book about werewolves! She had to find it again. Her cousin Hector went by with a handful of books, and Maddie grabbed him, sending them toppling to the floor. "Get out of the way!" he said crossly as she bent to shuffle through them. He kicked the one she reached for, sending it spinning away from her hands.

What am I doing? she thought in a frenzy. Father Mac had that book! He had it back near the houses, by the other fire. She turned and raced out again, skinning past men carrying a heavy chest down the stone steps, past Tom's Ma and Old Peggy arguing over a sewing kit. She ran to the fire by the bog, searching the ground for the book. Stools, distaffs, and baskets of wool lay abandoned on the ground where they had talked. Someone had dropped a half-knitted sock in the mud.

Black Ewan walked by on his way from the castle. Maddie saw him bend down and pick her book out of a clump of grass. Then he tossed it onto the glowing embers.

Maddie tried to retrieve it, but the heat forced her back. The book about werewolves. Paul's only hope for a cure. The pages curled and blackened and became licking flames, their secrets lost forever.

"That didn't belong to you!" she cried out in disappointment. The farmer just patted her on the shoulder.

"Maddie, you don't understand," he said, steering her toward the houses. "This is a problem for your elders."

Just like Paul, thought the girl bitterly. A problem for my elders. "And that's how elders solve problems, is it?" she challenged. "They throw them into the fire."

"We take care of our own," he replied. "We attack before we're attacked. One day you'll have people to protect, and then you'll understand."

I do have people to protect, thought Maddie. I have people to protect from you.

They came around the corner of Black Ewan's house. Colin the Smith knelt there, hammering on Mad Angus's fetter. The smith had taken off the padlock and was pounding an extra link into its place, forming an unbroken chain between the two prisoners so that the Englishman couldn't escape.

"Hey!" exclaimed Ned angrily. "Why do all this? The harvest is done, and we got no work now. We got to go."

Black Ewan bent down to pick up the padlock, eye to eye with the scruffy Traveler. "I'll deal with you later, you murderous scum," he promised grimly. "Did you think I'd let you walk away after you tried to kill my brother's boy?"

"That little villain?" sneered the old man. "If you beat manners into him, I wouldn't have to do it. Wish I hit you instead. I'll cave your skull in." Colin the Smith finished his work and picked up his tools, and he and Black Ewan walked away.

"Cursed meddle-maker!" fumed Ned. "Stupid

clod! No work now from that old woman, no money, no drink!" He jerked crossly on his chain, and Mad Angus jerked back harder. Ned abandoned the contest. "And what are you unhappy for?" he demanded irritably of Maddie. "You got a face like a pallbearer."

"Lady Mary was helping me," she told him sadly. "She was hunting for a cure for Paul. She had a book about it, but it's burned up. He'll never be cured now."

# 10

Maddie went home to find Fair Sarah building up the cooking fire and Paul fetching in peats. He dropped them by the hearth and came over to the girl. "Madeleine, what was it about?" he asked quietly.

Terribly discouraged and frightened at the transformation of her neighbors, Maddie wasn't ready to answer him. She gathered comfort from the familiar sights of her own house: the milk sheep lying in the corner, the chickens murmuring quietly to themselves as they roosted for the night. Then she looked at Paul, and her feeling of comfort evaporated. She knew just how the faces of the townspeople would look when they threw him onto the fire.

"Tell the truth, I don't know what it was about," she said, kneeling by her mother's side to help her pat out oatcakes. "Black Ewan says Lady Mary's a witch because of the smith's baby and because of the—the Water Horse that attacked you. But because of lots of other things, too, things that go back years and years. People were thinking them up all day."

"Well, I know what it was about, if you don't," sighed Fair Sarah. "Black Ewan's never forgiven that woman because Kathleen wouldn't marry him. Lady Mary had no kin to stand by her, and the people are afraid. They're looking for someone to blame right now. Strange things have been happening lately."

James Weaver and Father Mac had been watching over Lady Mary in the Hole until Black Ewan brought the padlock and secured the trapdoor. Then they had stayed by the castle to make sure that the crowd worked out its anger and no harm came to the prisoner. The two men ducked under the doorway now, and Father Mac bent to warm his hands.

"Is she really a witch?" asked the wood-carver, looking at Maddie.

"No!" she burst out in response. "She's a sharp-tongued, proud old woman, and that's all she is."

"But she'll die as a witch," growled Father Mac. "Of that I have no doubt. I can't just sit by while an innocent woman is hanged out of revenge and fear. I can't watch my parish commit murder."

"Do you have a choice, Father?" asked James Weaver. "You'll not find a way into the Hole, and Black Ewan will take his farmhands with him to escort her to the new lord. The padlock's on the grate over Lady Mary, and Black Ewan always has the key."

"It isn't right, what's happening to her," Maddie said in a pleading tone, and her eyes told Paul that she didn't know what to do. Would it save Lady Mary if she gave away his secret, or would it just mean another death?

A gloomy silence settled over the room. The young man sat down and took up his carving, frowning as he thought.

"I can make a key," he announced. They all stared blankly at him. "I can study Black Ewan's key," he explained, "and I can carve you a copy."

"A wooden key would break in the lock, son," observed Father Mac kindly.

"You'd have to have one cast, or have a smith study my key," answered Paul. "I've done work for smiths before, making models of broken tools."

"A model," breathed Father Mac. "Would Colin the Smith do the work, do you think?"

"He'd do it," said Fair Sarah. "My brother would do the work for me, and his own wife would never know."

Father Mac sat up straight, his eyes flashing. "Then make me that key," he said, "and I'll take care of the rest. I'll get their witch to safety."

"This is a serious matter," warned James Weaver. "If word got out that we helped Lady Mary escape, we'd be turned out of the town, and the lad here would face even worse than that."

Maddie discovered that Father Mac and her parents were looking gravely at her. "Oh, don't fret about me," she replied modestly. "I can keep a secret."

The next day was windy and cold, perfect for threshing. The men opened the wickerwork doors on either side of the grain barn and threshed out the grain on the open floor, beating the kernels from their seed heads with hinged flails while the women tossed the kernels in baskets so that the wind could blow away the chaff.

Threshing was hard work, and the men were soaked with sweat in spite of the cold. This was the sort of simple task that Mad Angus excelled at, and he threshed more than all the rest of them put together. Ned was almost no help at all, but Black Ewan saw to it that he took his turns.

The men had decided that the young wood-carver was too weak to do any threshing, so they brought him tools to mend instead. Paul sat on the edge of the threshing floor with the broken tools around him.

"That's a fine job, lad," remarked Black Ewan, wiping his damp brow and sitting down beside the carver after his turn with the flail. "It's good to see you busy at useful work."

Paul didn't say a word to his unsuspecting model, but he sneaked long and careful glances at the big skeleton key around his neck. He was not so foolish as to fashion a key right in front of the farmer, but every now and then he took out a small block of wood and made a nick in it to guide his carving later.

After lunch, Paul returned to the weaver's house

and sat down by the door, where he had the best light. He sat there for hours, almost without moving, deeply engrossed in his task. Hurrying back and forth as she went about her own work, Maddie watched the carver. She remembered her first view of him the day the Travelers had come. He had sat just so, with his shaggy black hair falling into his face and the shavings falling onto his knees. Except that this time he glanced up to smile at her and held out the finished key. Her heart skipped a beat as she smiled back.

"You're done already? You're that cunning," she exclaimed, studying the wooden key. "Black Ewan himself couldn't tell the difference."

"I just hope it works," he said, taking it back to examine it. "It's as close as I know how to make it."

The threshing days passed, full of hard work and high spirits. The witch still huddled in her dark, rocky cell. Maddie came home from Mass one morning to find that Paul had been out in the biting wind gathering eggs for her, and her mother was scolding him as she fixed breakfast. The chickens weren't laying as they had in high summer, and the sheep were giving less milk. It was the turn of the year toward the lean times.

After breakfast, Fair Sarah left with some broth for Tom's Ma. Maddie was just picking up her knitting and settling down to keep the fire when she noticed something odd. Her apple tree that Paul had carved wasn't where she had left it. She went over and picked it up.

The wooden figure was different. It still had a tree's crown of leaves and apples, but the trunk had turned into a pale, slim girl. Leaves grew out of her hair, and her two arms stretched out to become branches. Maddie walked toward the doorway and turned the carving in the light, studying it with wonder.

"It's you," said a voice from the doorway, and she looked up to find Paul there. "At least, it looks like you," he added awkwardly. "Do you like it? I had just finished it that first morning when I looked up and saw you talking to Ned, and then I looked down and saw you in the wood. That's why I didn't want to give it to you when you asked to buy it. Because I wanted to carve what I had seen."

Maddie examined it. The tree girl was slender and sweet, poised and graceful. Maddie could see that she was happy by the lift of her arms and her chin. Happy to be an apple tree, happy to grow where she was planted. The tip of one toe-root just showed beneath her long skirt.

"After I saw you," he went on, "every block of wood I saw had you inside it. I carved you instead of working on the box I was supposed to finish, and that's why we stayed so long. I carved you so many times, Ned swore at me. He said I was going soft in the head."

"But why would you carve me? Who would want to see me?" Maddie held out the tree girl. "Just me, I'm not fancy like this."

Paul took the carving to look at it and then at her. She could tell that somehow he still saw the resemblance.

"You're beautiful, Madeleine," he said simply.

"Beautiful? Me? Lord bless your heart, I'm not beautiful! With my round face, and these big hands—" She held them out. "And I'm thick in the middle like Ma, all us women in my family are thick in the waist; why, just look at my aunt Janet, and even Bess has already gotten thick."

The young carver waited until she stopped babbling. Then he handed back the apple tree with a frown. "You are, too, beautiful," he retorted with perfect sincerity, and perhaps he was right after all.

Threshing was over at last. Everyone gathered in Black Ewan's big house for a feast, and young roosters who had walked tall in their pride suddenly found the promise of life cut short. Maddie looked around the smoky room at her neighbors chatting and singing and realized that Paul wasn't there. She went hunting for him and found him out in the twilight, carving a two-handled drinking cup.

"Come join us," she said, but the young man shook his head. She knelt down to study the graceful cup. "Please, Paul. Have a little fun for once. You're among friends here."

"I'm not among friends," he answered. "I can't ever be. They wouldn't be my friends if they knew."

"Well, if you don't want them to know, you should come join us," remarked the sensible girl. "They all know you can talk, and they think it's strange that you don't. If you miss an evening like this, they'll gossip about you."

So Paul came into the house, bringing his carving with him, and he sat in a corner under a little rush light to finish the two-handled cup. The others welcomed him with friendly words, and Maddie felt she had won a victory. Little Ian was just finishing a tale about Finn Mac Cumhail and the founding of his warrior band.

"The king released the three hundred heroes who were condemned to die, and he gave them all to Finn," he concluded. "You never saw such a host! The sunlight glittered off their shields and long spears and the gold collars and armbands they wore. One by one, they knelt at Finn's feet, and they swore faith with him for all time. From that day forth, they roamed the land looking for enemies, and one man among them could conquer a whole army. They were the bright-haired Fianna, the most beautiful of warriors, and all the people rejoiced in their brave deeds."

The listeners murmured their approval at this familiar ending, and Little Ian paused for a drink. "Why doesn't the carver lad give us a story," he proposed. "Come, we know you can speak, and the old man's not here to beat you. Tell us a tale of your own people."

Paul gave Maddie a look that said as clearly as words *This is your fault,* but she just gave him an encouraging smile in return. He turned the cup in his hands, agitated, before glancing at the spectators lining the long room.

"My own people," he murmured, and he looked at the cup again. He took a deep breath.

"A young chief was hunting in the woods," he began, "and he heard merry singing far from any house. He followed the sound and saw a lovely maiden walking through the forest. Her eyes were gray like storm clouds, and her hair was yellow like grain, and no sooner had he seen her than he loved her. He stepped up to her and would have greeted her kindly, but she turned and ran from him.

"The chief followed her to a tall, round tower. He would have gone into the tower after her, but an old woman barred his way. 'Where has she gone?' he demanded. 'And what bride price will you have for her? I want to make her my wife.'

"'There will be no bride price for my daughter, and no bride,' the old hag told him. 'It's said that men will be her doom.'

"But the chief wouldn't take this for an answer. 'Name a bride price,' he declared, 'and name it now, because if you don't, I'll come with my strong men and take her away from here and make her my wife anyway.' Then the old woman sighed and thought, and at last she asked that her daughter come back to stay with her in the tower for one week out of every four, and to this price the young chief agreed.

"The pair were married and lived happily, and the maiden bore her husband twin sons. He was terribly proud of his beautiful wife until his kinsman came to visit.

"'Where's this beauty I've heard you boasting about?' demanded the kinsman, and he laughed when he learned she was not at home. 'Cousin, someone is leading you by the nose like a bull,' he said. 'If you asked me what I think, I'd say that your wife has two husbands instead of one.'

"That night the young chief paced his house in anger and suspicion. At last he journeyed through the woods and crept up to the round tower. Fearful shrieks and noises came from inside it. He climbed the vines that covered it to look in a high window. There sat the old hag, knitting and humming, with his two baby sons sleeping by her side. But his lovely wife was nowhere to be seen. In her place was a hideous monster.

"It looked like—like—" Paul broke off, his voice unsteady. "I don't know what it looked like. But it was big and black like a shadow, an evil thing that thought only of harm. It was chained to the wall, and it tore at the chain and hissed and shrieked foul curses. The forest rang with the sound of its screams.

"The chief beat down the door and killed the old hag with one stroke of his sword. But he sat down before the ghastly monster and watched it fling itself to and fro. He waited all through that long night, until dawn finally came, and at the end of the chain, asleep, lay his own lovely wife.

"Then the chief brought stones and mortar to the tower, and he walled up his wife inside it, and his two young sons in there with her. The last thing he saw as he placed the final stone was the babies sitting by their sleeping mother and playing with her beautiful yellow hair."

The listeners stirred and scratched their heads, thinking about the story. Maddie sat still in horror. Paul stared down at his carving, working furiously. The knife seemed to fly in his hands.

"He did a good day's work, I'm thinking," considered Old Peggy. "Can't leave a creature like that to roam loose."

"He'd have done better to stop her mouth with mud and drown her in the sea," proposed Tom's Ma, "and not let her remain on the land."

"He'd have done better to burn her," opined Little Ian, "and scatter her ashes over the water. That's quite a tale, lad. So you say that the chief was one of your people?"

But Maddie knew it wasn't the chief that Paul counted as kin. She spoke quickly before he could answer.

"I don't believe that story!" she exclaimed passionately. "It can't be true. No one could do that to someone he loved, or to his own children, either."

"It's true, Madeleine," he said grimly, his eyes on his work. "I've seen the tower without a door, and that's where I learned the story."

"Don't take it so much to heart, child," said Father Mac to Maddie. "That's a very old tale from the days before we had Christ's Church and His grace. Evil things like that belong to the pagan world, when ignorant people still offered sacrifices to the demons and studied the flights of birds."

Paul gave a gasp as his knife slipped and gashed him deep in the thumb. The blood flowed over the wooden cup and soaked into the freshly carved surface. Maddie thought of his mother killing chickens and praying to the gods. So it was something worse than nonsense, after all, and his face showed her that he knew it. He stared without moving at the ruined cup, at the dark stains on the light wood. Then he tossed it into the peat fire and watched as it began to smoke.

That night Maddie dreamed that she stood just outside the castle with food for Lady Mary. Someone inside was sobbing and crying. Underfoot on the stone threshold was a long, brown smear. It hadn't been there before.

The crying rose into screams and wails and burst into bellows and groans. It was soulless, the sound of neither laughter nor tears. Maddie peered past the stone steps into the deep gloom of the building, looking for something she knew. Large, dim shapes dangled there like dead beasts waiting to be butchered, and that sobbing, screaming thing was coming toward her.

The next instant, Maddie sat up in bed. She was safe at home. She lay back down, heart pounding, and thought about the awful dream. Before, the castle had been the home of a proud, interesting old woman. Now it was a place of suffering and despair. Soon Lady Mary would be gone from the rocky cell, and the bleak castle would be empty. The new lord planned to put one of his strong men there, but Maddie knew something even stronger. Something that screamed. Something that killed. Something that might be looking for a home.

# 11

The hush of dawn lay over the valley. Then the hush was broken. Maddie woke to the sound of Gillies yelling for his master and Black Ewan calling back. Her father scrambled past, climbing out of the box bed and ducking under the door frame on his way out of the house. Maddie bumped into Paul in the darkness, and Fair Sarah threw her kerchief over her braid. They wrapped their blankets around themselves as they hurried out into the morning.

The dim, dark gray of a cold mist lay over the houses. From all directions in the fog came voices calling, asking, and answering, and someone lit a rush light, spreading a meager glow. They saw excited faces in the pool of light, and black silhouettes against it.

"The witch is gone!" cried Gillies. "The Hole is still locked up tight, but she's nowhere inside. I tried the padlock. It didn't budge."

"But I have the key!" exclaimed Black Ewan, reaching for it and holding it up.

"She's walked through the stone," guessed Horse.

"She's been snatched off to hell," suggested Little Ian. A wild babble ensued, and it was impossible to learn anything from the result.

All that foggy day, the town was like an overturned hive. The men strode resolutely out into the swirling gray gloom and were swallowed up in it, calling to each other as they lost their bearings. The dogs found Lady Mary's trail and followed it out of the castle to the loch shore, but no one found the tiniest sign of the witch. She had evidently walked right into the lake. The Water Horse had taken her home.

That night Father Mac sat by the weaver's peat fire. "It went well," he told them, "in spite of the weather. Your key worked nicely." He nodded at

Paul. "I took Little Ian's fishing boat and rowed her across the loch. Then I brought back the boat and swilled it with water to put off the dogs.

"Getting home across the loch was a bit of a trick. The fog was solid by then, and not a breath stirred; the water was like black glass. I thought I'd never get across. I thought I was rowing in circles. She's with a friend of mine, and he'll see that she's safe. You'd best keep this for a few days, James," he added, taking out the key. "Hide it somewhere till Colin goes out on his next trip around the settlements. Then he can take it with him and melt it down.

"She cried and cried, poor thing," he said sadly. "She cried the whole time. She said it wasn't the hanging, it was the torture she couldn't bear. She said she'd seen what torture did, how it changed people into animals, and she was so afraid of that happening to her."

"When has Lady Mary seen torture?" wondered Maddie.

"I didn't ask her," said the priest, "but I have an idea. That book Black Ewan handed me had a name in it. It used to belong to a brilliant scholar from a well-known family, quite a rising star among the clergy when I was young, and the darling of the university until his ideas became too wild. Then there was a scandal, and they investigated him, and he fled to the Continent. Shortly afterward, he was burned at the stake for heresy.

"Lady Mary would have been a young woman then, and she must have been part of the clergyman's scandal. She probably followed him to Europe and saw what happened to him. She couldn't have come back to the city after such behavior; her family wouldn't have taken her in. The new lord's wife was probably the only friend she had left."

Maddie stared into the fire, remembering the look in Lady Mary's eyes when she had mentioned burning. That haunted, desolate look. No wonder Lady Mary had kept so much to herself and had had so little patience with God and neighbor.

The townspeople were frightened and dismayed by their witch's disappearance. No one wanted to mention Lady Mary by name—that might be unlucky—but no one could think of anything else, either. She might know who had taken her sewing kit or who had kept her silver necklace. Perhaps she would come to their hearths at night and draw a fatal charm in the ashes. Or she might have managed to escape to the new lord and told him what had happened to all that valuable furniture. He might take Lady Mary's part against them because they had acted so rashly and not consulted him first.

A feeling of melancholy settled over the town, leaving its people surly and out of sorts. They were like a man waking up after a drinking binge, a little afraid of what had been done, and resentful about the fear. Most resentful of all was Black Ewan. He stalked about his work looking like a thundercloud, and the people knew his temper well enough to leave him alone. All but one, that is.

"Hey!" called Ned as the farmer passed. The Traveler and Mad Angus were at work mending the earthen dyke under the watchful eye of Horse. During the year, it had slumped in spots, and Mad Angus was industriously shoveling it back up again, his whole front covered in mud.

"Hey! I hear you got a witch you can't lay a hand on," jeered the Traveler. "You people make me laugh, the whole lot of you sent on a dance by one little woman."

"Maybe you know something about it," said the farmer, although he knew it was highly unlikely.

"Maybe I do," retorted the old man with a grin.

"Maybe I saw you let her out with that great big key, and kiss her good-bye, too."

"You filthy liar," growled Black Ewan, grabbing him by the tunic and shaking him like a dog. "Threshing's over and done. It's time I dealt with you."

"You can't deal with a woman, how you going to deal with me?" taunted Ned. "Take more than you to scare me. Wish I'd let her out. I'd have did it to see the stupid look on your face."

"You lying, murdering drunkard!" shouted Black Ewan. "That witch got away from me, but you won't. We'll lock you in the Hole tonight to see if the hell-fiends let you out. And tomorrow morning, I'm going to kill you."

Horse climbed to his feet and stared at his master, and Gillies came over the dyke, his spade in his hand. Ned rubbed his whiskered chin thoughtfully, a twinkle in his faded eyes.

"What do you say to that?" demanded the enraged farmer.

"Wish I had my staff," responded the old man. "I'd whip you proper, you yapping pup."

Word spread like wildfire through the town that the Traveler was to be killed at dawn.

"You'll not let him die like that," Maddie challenged her family, but no one spoke in reply. Her father was winding yarn onto his shuttles. Her mother was stirring up the fire. Paul stood by the door with his back to the rest of them. She hadn't seen his face since they'd heard.

"You can't mean you'll leave that poor man to die!" she insisted. "He doesn't have to. You have the key."

"Maddie, that's a secret," said her mother. "You're not to talk of it." So many secrets. Maddie was sick of them.

"Black Ewan's no fool," said her father seriously. "He thinks someone can get into the Hole, and he's watching for it. If that key is found, there'll be more than one death. Paul here will be the next to go."

"But there has to be a way," Maddie protested miserably. "Ned's important. Paul needs him."

The young carver turned around and looked at her, a warning glittering in his eyes. Maddie felt the sting of it, and a lump rose in her throat. She wrapped her blanket around herself and ran past him out into the rain.

"Father Mac!" she called at the door of his little cottage, and the priest looked up and waved her in. "They won't do anything for Ned," she exclaimed, warming up before the hearth. "Paul and my dad, they won't help him because Dad says Black Ewan will be waiting for them."

Father Mac sat for a short time in silence. "Your father's right," he said finally. "Black Ewan's probably hoping we'll be fool enough to try again."

"But Ned doesn't deserve to die!" she protested. "He's just like Lady Mary."

"No, young Madeleine, you're wrong," replied the priest. "Ned really did what he's accused of. He beat a child, and he almost killed him. Men have died for less."

"He had to!" insisted Maddie.

"And why's that?" asked Father Mac. But Maddie remembered the look in Paul's eyes. She couldn't tell him.

"So you'll not do anything, either?" she demanded fiercely. "You're letting him die, too."

"Here's something the young don't think of," answered the priest. "We all of us have to die. This life is just a test to see what sort of person you'll be, whether you'll be honest and faithful or wicked and mean. The hardships that come with it are part of the test, and at the end of it, we die. Folk worry about that overmuch. They can't see beyond the grave. But there's a life beyond this one, the life that we prepare for ourselves while we're here."

"Then I'm minded Black Ewan is preparing a hot one," snapped Maddie. "First Lady Mary, and now this. It's cruel to send an old man to his death."

"I'm worried about Black Ewan myself," sighed the priest. "Tell the truth, I'm more worried for him than for Ned. Don't take it so hard, lass. There's all kinds of ways to die, and we each of us face one of them sooner or later."

Maddie left the priest's cottage meekly enough, but she was in no way resigned to letting Ned die. She knew where her father had put the key, and she resolved to rescue the Traveler alone. That afternoon, she walked to the castle to see him, right past Gillies and Black Ewan, who were standing guard outside. She knelt down by the Hole and looked in.

It was dark by the trapdoor of the little prison, and pitch-black inside it. Ned's face appeared below the barred grate, ghostly in the dim light.

"Evening, miss," said the old man just as cheerfully as if he weren't condemned to die.

"Evening, Ned," replied Maddie in a low voice. "Is anyone in there with you?"

Ned rubbed his bristly chin. "Couple of rats, maybe," he guessed. "Couple of louse, maybe. Why?"

"I can get you out of here," she announced excitedly. "I'm meaning to set you free."

"So you're the one that done it?" He chuckled. "I might have knowed it was you, you got a hand in every pie roundabouts. Well, it ain't like springing a trap this time. Old meddle is watching. Best save your kind works for the poor and leave me where I be."

"But I can't!" said Maddie urgently. She hadn't expected resistance from this quarter. "You have to escape! Paul needs you. You can't let him down."

The old man scratched his dirty tunic and stared at the walls of his cell. He said nothing for a long time.

"I was away when my boy was bit," he began, as if talking to himself. "Away working the harvest for my own lord. I come home to find my wife and babies died and my boy mortal sick. The folk of him that done it, they took us in with them, and we traveled together for years. They learned me how to manage my boy. What to do and where to go. There's hidden places all over this land—old, old places. Places with a chain to them for to chain up the wolf when it's time. That's what we did, we travels up and we travels down, following the ways, visiting the places. That's how a wolf's got to live.

"I watched my boy so sick, I watched him change, the life leak out of him drop by drop. I was just as keen as you be, I was going to save him. I was going to cure my boy. Everywhere we go, I'd find the wise and the weird, the saints and the witch hags, and I asked them all. What do I do? How do I do it? What's the cure for his bite? I learned it, too, at long last, and a hard road behind, but it's when I learned that the road got really hard. Because I couldn't do it. Couldn't work the cure. It was too much for me."

So there was a cure! Maddie tensed in excitement, but the old man was still speaking. She held her breath to stop herself from interrupting him.

"My boy was a man now, a man with no man's life. Month after month I watched him change, and I done nothing about it. I took to drink beforehand to give me courage for the cure, and I took to drink after because I always hadn't done it, and I took to drink most times because I didn't want to see his eyes, my wife's blue eyes with that hunted look in them." He paused, and Maddie remembered the hunted look in Paul's eyes. No matter what he was doing, it never went away.

"Well, one time I go to drink," continued Ned, "and I say, This time is it. But I drank too much this time. I'm drunk, and I fell asleep. My boy got loose because I wasn't by to help. When I seen that chain empty on the ground, I sat right down and cried. But you know, I didn't go out after him. I stayed right where I be. It was the one safe place that night, you know, the one place where he wouldn't come back to.

"In the morning I found my boy crying over his dead, and we, both of us, we knew he can't live after that, not with what he seen and what he done. Me, I didn't want to live, neither, it's all my fault, you know. I let him down, let down my boy, all those years I knew what to do, and I never, ever done it. But me, I had to live, I had the young lad now to think on. I had to learn him the ways, same as was done for me. So we leave my boy and burn the place, and I looked after the lad." His voice became harsh and final. "But curing him, oh, no, that's never been my aim! Not if I ain't done it for my own boy."

"There's a cure!" exclaimed Maddie, interrupting at last. "What is it? Tell me! I have to know!"

The Traveler studied her in the dim light. "You have to, do you?" he said dryly. "Ready to go old Ned one better? There ain't nobody you wouldn't save."

"Tell me," she pleaded. "I want to help him. How can I cure him?"

"It's simple," he said in a low voice. "No trick to it. Anyone can do it. You wait till he's changed. Then you give yourself over to the wolf, all of your own free will. You walk right up so he can tear you apart and kill you and eat you. That's all you got to do."

Maddie stared at him with her mouth open. She couldn't even speak.

"And that's what I never done, God help me," he whispered. "Not to save my own poor boy. You let me be, now, young missy, with your saving and your curing. I don't want to be saved. I done the best I can by the lad, and you'll take care of him now. That meddling farmer, he's detestable and all, but he ain't really mean. He'll make it quick for me tomorrow, and me, I'm glad to go."

Maddie didn't realize she was crying until she was back outside the castle. She stood in the rain by the loch shore and cried and cried, and she didn't care that the men were watching.

# 12

Father Mac stayed that night down by the Hole. Black Ewan was keeping watch, and he complained about it.

"Stop singing songs!" he said irritably. "You sound like a catfight, and I don't see what that has to do with preparing a soul for death."

"Ah, lad," rumbled the big priest cheerfully, "just you hope there's someone to sing with you when your time comes."

Early next morning, the townspeople gathered outside the castle. The older ones remembered the dawn executions of former years, when their chief had lived there with his family and warriors. Maddie was too young. She didn't remember the busy times, when the castle was a place of power. She knew only the quiet little settlement that had remained when the fight for the land was over.

Black Ewan went into the castle with his three farmhands while the quiet crowd waited outside. They heard the grinding and clanking of the trapdoor and then indistinct voices within. After a time, the farmer reappeared, his execution finished. His men dragged the body of Ned out behind him.

Father Mac emerged, too, and he walked over to Maddie and her parents.

"He made a good end," said the priest in a low voice. "He confessed his sins and had the Last Rites of the Church. That's something to think of, young Madeleine. The best thing we can do in life is be ready for our own death."

Maddie wasn't listening to this consoling speech. She was staring at the castle doorway. A wide track of blood crossed the stone threshold. It matched the brown smear she had seen in her dream.

"Hey, now!" called out the priest. "That's not necessary!"

At work over the sprawled body, Black Ewan didn't reply. He was hacking the head off the old

Traveler. Horse and Gillies brought up a long ladder and leaned it against the castle where a thick beam jutted from the wall overhead. The farmer tied a knot in Ned's greasy gray hair, climbed the rungs, and hung the head from a hook on the bottom of the beam.

"I protest!" said Father Mac indignantly. "This isn't a legal execution, and we don't need that kind of pagan display."

Black Ewan climbed back down the ladder and looked up to study his handiwork. What the head meant to him he couldn't exactly say, but he felt a deep satisfaction at the sight. His distant ancestors had returned from battle with such heads slung about their necks and belts, convinced that they owned the souls of those dead enemies.

Mouth and eyes open, the head of the old man stared vacantly out over the crowd. It swayed in the breeze and turned a little, hanging from its knotted hair. Blood rimmed the dark neck and dripped sluggishly to the ground. Watching those drops soak into the earth, Maddie felt decidedly ill. Whenever they passed that place, the townspeople scuffed a cross into the dirt with a toe. She herself had done it since she was a small child. Now she finally understood the reason. Human blood fell there and had fallen there many, many times before. As long as the castle had stood, heads had hung from that beam and dripped onto the cross-marked ground.

A loud cry rose from behind them, like the bellow of a cow that had lost her calf. The whole crowd turned around to see. Mad Angus shuffled forward, bleating and wailing. Tears ran into the madman's filthy beard as he lifted the corpse of his comrade in chains. He sank down onto the ground to cradle it, howling with grief.

There, you see what you've done with your meddling, thought Maddie angrily. She looked around for Black Ewan, but the farmer was already walking away with his men. Father Mac stepped forward instead.

"Come along, Angus," he said to the weeping giant. "Let's get him buried as well as we can."

While the rest of the town followed their priest away to the churchyard, Paul returned to Maddie's house. She lingered outside to wait for him. The young man emerged carrying a sack and a small carving of the Madonna.

"You'll give this to your mother for me, won't you?" he asked, handing the carving to her.

"You're leaving!" she gasped. He didn't answer. Instead, he walked away. Maddie hurried after him.

"But you can't leave!" she cried as they reached the path that ran along the loch shore. "Ma will be so upset, you not saying good-bye, and we haven't buried Ned yet, you should stay to pray for him."

Paul didn't slow down. "I don't think my prayers would help any," he said. "You do it for me, Madeleine. You're better at it than I am."

"You can't go," she repeated desperately as they came to the rotten stump. "You know you can't! You need my help—for the next time."

The young wood-carver stopped and looked around carefully before he looked at her.

"I'll be as far from here as I can be before the next time," he said. "Don't worry. I'll manage it somehow. Maybe I'll take a boat out onto the water, or maybe out to sea. I don't think I could get out of one when I'm changed."

"You'll drown, surely," she protested.

"That's no loss," he replied.

"When will you come back?" Maddie demanded.

The young man looked at the high hills across

the loch. They were starting to turn golden and tan in the frosty nights.

"I won't ever come back here," he answered.

Maddie took a deep breath. "Then I'm coming with you."

Paul actually hesitated. Then his face grew grim. "That would be a fine return I'd make for all your parents' kindness."

"But I promised Ned!" she exclaimed in distress. "I have to look after you." This was such a stupid thing to say to a grown man that Maddie blushed deeply, but the carver's face softened as he looked down at hers.

"I'd like that," he admitted quietly. "I wish you could have. If things had only been different."

"If things had been different," she echoed miserably, staring at the ground.

"Good-bye, Madeleine. I'll not forget you."

Maddie didn't know what to say. "Good-bye, Paul," she whispered.

"And you'll be careful for my sake?" he asked earnestly. "On the full-moon nights? And sometimes, when you're praying for Ned, maybe you could pray for me."

Maddie nodded, and Paul walked off down the path by the shore of the quiet loch. She stood and watched him until he was out of sight. Then, dull and dreary with grief, she went home to tell her mother.

# 13

Fair Sarah took the news very hard and shed tears over her poor boy. She fretted and worried that night as stars shone down in the black sky and bitter frost gripped the empty fields. He still wasn't well. He wasn't strong. Where would he go in such weather, and with hardly a blanket to cover him?

Maddie's own sorrow left her bad-tempered and out of sorts. Many times a day, as she was doing her chores, she looked for Paul and missed him. Somehow, he would try to manage his ghastly illness without her. Somewhere as far from her as he could possibly be.

As the next few days passed, her mood didn't lighten. She should at least feel glad that the town was free of that hellish creature, the shadow that lived inside Paul, but as she ran her errands, she couldn't help seeing the dark brown smear across the castle doorway. It had appeared right out of her nightmare, like a promise of evil to come.

The old Traveler made things far worse for the girl. His head still dangled from the castle beam, and no predators came near it. It exerted an influence that Maddie could feel even from far away, a raising of the hair on the back of her neck and a prickling along her skin. It seemed to be watching her. Wherever she went, she could feel the force of that gaze, and she couldn't stop herself from looking back. And every time she looked, no matter where she was standing, the head was facing her.

"It's just my fancy," decided the girl, with an attempt at her habitual good sense. "The wind shakes the dead thing around, that's all, and I happen to look up at the wrong moment."

Stopping on the loch shore, she deliberately stared at the head, hanging from its long hair, and received in return the full force of those sunken, opaque eyes. She walked past it over to the path through the bog, watching all the while. The head swiveled slowly as she went by.

Terrified, Maddie raced up the path to the houses and threw herself into a group of startled townspeople. Father Mac was there, and she caught him by the hands.

"The Traveler's head is watching me, Father!" she sobbed to the priest. "It never lets me out of its sight!"

Father Mac immediately stormed off to find Black Ewan. "Get that head down from there so we can bury it properly!" he ordered. "It's doing the devil's work."

The next morning, Fair Sarah reached into the salt box and found it empty. "Maddie, do you go down to the salt barrel in the castle and fill this up again."

The girl started off with a willing spirit down the path through the bog. She slowed as she reached the castle doorway. No creature screamed from within the gloomy space, but there was the brown stain across the stone step where Ned had been dragged out, and there in the dust was a cross where his blood had fallen. Above was the hook where his head had hung. She glanced up at the beam.

A force seemed to strike her and run through her, setting the blood singing in her ears. The head still dangled from the beam. It wasn't gone after all. It didn't look like it had before. It looked very much alive. It gazed down at her with those faded blue eyes, and it wore a broad grin.

Maddie couldn't move. She felt as if she were floating. "You aren't supposed to be here," she whispered to the head. "You're supposed to be gone from here."

The Traveler's head seemed to be listening. It looked as if it could speak. It grinned cheerfully down at her and gave a conspiratorial wink.

With a shriek, Maddie turned and ran down the shoreline away from the ghastly thing. She found Little Ian mending sails beside his boat and collapsed next to him, hiding behind the keel.

"The Traveler's head!" she exclaimed when she could talk. "It looked at me again!"

Little Ian pulled the yarn through his torn sail and glanced up at the castle critically. "That old thing was buried yesterday," he said.

Maddie sat trembling, thinking about this. "That's just what I told it," she answered. Cautiously, she raised herself until she could see the castle beam. Nothing hung there now.

"I'm telling you, it was there!" she declared breathlessly, sitting back down. "I saw it just like I'm seeing you."

"I'm not saying you didn't," remarked Little Ian calmly. "Don't be so upset. Heads, now, they're not such a bad thing. It's good luck to have a head about."

Maddie rubbed her hands together to stop their shaking. "It is?" she ventured faintly.

"Oh, aye," said the fisherman, a gleam in his dark little eyes. "A head looks after a place. It guards it, you might say. And don't forget, that old man's the Churchyard Watcher till someone else gets buried. He has a job to do, for once in his life."

Maddie remembered the stories about the Churchyard Watcher. When someone died, his soul stayed in the churchyard to guard it until he could call his replacement, the next one to die. If no one died for a long time, people felt sorry for the last one buried, who had to keep such a long watch before going off to his reward.

"Did he say anything?" Little Ian wanted to know. "They say heads can be powerfully wise."

"No. He looked like he might, but he just grinned and winked."

Little Ian grew glum and put down his needle. "Well, that's a bad thing," he sighed. "There's only one reason that lazy criminal would be so pleased, and that's because his time as Watcher is already up. There's going to be a death soon."

"Then I'll be next!" gasped Maddie. "Why else would he show himself to me?"

"Now, I'm not so sure of that," mused Little Ian, looking at her thoughtfully. "They do say the Watcher is supposed to tap you on the shoulder if you're next. Of course," he added reluctantly, "a foreigner like him might not know the right way to go about it."

Forgetting her mother's salt box by the shore, Maddie ran to find Father Mac. He was standing on the low step of the stone church, looking out over his little domain. Torn racks of clouds huddled over the town, and the blue-gray smoke percolating out of the humped houses drifted up to join them. "The weather's breaking up," announced the big priest cheerfully. "We'll have a fine, warm day for this time of year."

"Father, I'm going to die!" said Maddie. "I need the Last Rites of the Church."

The priest listened to her story about the head and its unwelcome interest. "By rights, he ought to tap me on the shoulder," she concluded anxiously. "But Little Ian says maybe he doesn't know that since he's ignorant of our ways."

Father Mac peered thoughtfully up at the tattered clouds. "I don't know everything about the world," he remarked, "but I do know that no one stays behind in the churchyard after he dies. We go before God to be judged as soon as our souls leave our bodies. It's the demons that try to keep these old notions alive. There's been evil here, and strange doings lately. I think the demons are playing tricks."

"You mean a demon grinned at me?" she demanded. "But surely that's even worse!" She had had a certain amount of experience recently with such creatures, and she could imagine what would make a demon look pleased.

"I'm just saying that we don't know what it means," countered Father Mac. "Maybe it's only trying to scare you. I'll come bless the place and exorcise the demon, and I'll give you my blessing, too. But I certainly don't think you need the Last Rites." He went into the church and returned with his book, a candle, and a flask of holy water.

"Do you see that?" he demanded triumphantly, pointing at the clouds with one thick finger. "There's the very first patch of blue sky. You watch, young Madeleine, we'll have clear skies today, and a fine view of the full moon tonight."

"Tonight's the full moon!" breathed Maddie in horror. "Oh, no! I am going to die!"

All day long, as the weather turned warm and the clouds broke up, Maddie thought about the full moon. Be careful, Paul had said. And the old Traveler, giving her that friendly wink, as if they had shared a joke. You know what's going to happen, the head had told her.

Maddie looked down at the lengthening shadows, remembering the black thing before her door. Out of the whole town of people, it had come to kill her. Maybe she wasn't supposed to be the next Churchyard Watcher. Then again, maybe she was. She had little chance against demons and shadows, but she could do one thing. When they came looking for her, she could make herself a little harder to find.

"Bess," she said to her cousin, "let's stay in the barn tonight."

Bess was wild at the idea of getting out of her crowded house. The proper permissions were quickly sought and given. Dusk fell, and their chores were over. They unlatched one wickerwork door of the grain barn and pulled it shut behind them.

The barn was made of lattice panels on three sides. Maddie had chosen it for her hiding place because she could see anything that was coming and because it had two doors. It was stuffed full of oat straw left over from the threshing. The girls made cozy nests for themselves, disrupting several families of mice that had done the same, and settled down to an evening of gossip.

"I brought a sieve," announced Bess, "so we can tell our fortunes."

"Father Mac says that's nonsense," observed Maddie.

"Old Peggy told me she did it, and she saw her future husband first thing in the morning." Bess giggled. "He'd been waiting all night by the door because she told him she was trying the sieve."

When the moon rose and the time was right, Bess produced that object and chanted over it the rhyme that promised her a sight of the man she would marry. "Now you do it," she directed, passing the sieve to Maddie.

"I don't want to," replied the girl. Father Mac

frowned on such things, so it might jeopardize her soul. She wanted to be prepared for death if it came that night. Besides, she had become pessimistic recently on the subject of marriage.

"Oh, please," begged her cousin. "I want to see what happens. I've always wondered if it would really work."

"How is it supposed to work?" demanded Maddie reasonably. "We're both right here, so we'll see the same man first thing in the morning. We can't both marry the same man, can we? Father Mac would knock our heads together."

"We'll have a footrace, and whoever tags him first gets him," proposed Bess. "I always could run faster than you."

Maddie sighed and worked the little charm, sieving three sieves full of nothing. "I did it," she grumbled, passing it back. "But I didn't want to."

"Now, you have to tell me faithfully who you see first in the morning," said her cousin. "No matter how awful it is. Maybe it'll be Black Ewan. He's never been married, you know."

"Ugh," muttered Maddie. "I'd not marry him." She remembered the farmer washing old Ned's blood from his hands.

"I hope I see Thomas," said Bess dreamily, combing out her black hair and peering through the latticework wall to watch the rising moon. "Last year he was just bones, but not anymore."

"He's looked worse," agreed Maddie, watching her. She had always admired Bess's hair.

"I'm thinking Gillies has his eye on you," Bess continued. "And him such a good worker, he could have a house of his own if he wanted."

Maddie sighed, braiding her hair to keep it from tangling while she slept.

Bess turned to look at her, black stripes falling across her face as the moon rose on the other side of the wickerwork. "I'm thinking you lost your heart to that carver boy," she remarked critically. "He's worked a spell over you."

"He has," agreed Maddie unhappily. "It's a shame I couldn't return the favor."

She fell asleep at last, watching the bright clouds through the wickerwork and wondering where Paul was. When she woke up, she knew where he was: standing outside in the moonlight. He had come back to her. But he hadn't come back as Paul.

# 14

The people in the town woke up at the same instant and held their breath at the same time. They listened to the short, sharp, frantic screams, becoming ragged with pain and terror. A gap of silence followed, more terrible than the sounds. Then another scream rose into the night.

Chilling, menacing, sharper than knives, the scream shivered on the quiet air. It hung over the houses for a long moment, holding every listener spellbound. No one who had heard it before could ever possibly forget it, and every one of them had heard it before.

"Maddie, what do we do?" sobbed Bess, the

straw rustling as she sat up, but Maddie caught her cousin in a tight grip.

"Don't make a sound," she breathed in Bess's ear, and she put her hand over her cousin's mouth.

Some distance away, the girls heard their priest by his cottage, speaking words in the sacred tongue. "Black Ewan, Colin, James," he shouted next, "there's someone needing our help."

"Someone beyond our help, I'm thinking." That was the smith's voice, coming from his house.

"Daddy," whimpered Bess, pushing the hand away. "Maddie, let's go."

But Maddie heard something else, something that only she had heard before: a snuffling, bubbling sound. It was circling the houses, coming toward the barn. Bess stirred in surprise, turning toward Maddie, but Maddie clapped her hand over her cousin's mouth again before Bess could ask what it was.

The air grew frigid as the creature approached, slobbering as it came. *"Blood, blood,"* it was bubbling softly to itself in a singsong chant of glee. Then it stopped outside the barn's woven door, and its song changed to a growl. *"Warm blood,"* it snarled. The wickerwork snapped in a splintering crash.

The two girls huddled in the straw and prayed

without making a sound. A confident note rang out in the darkness. A cock was greeting the dawn. The unnatural thing heard it, and it stopped in mid-snarl.

"*Morning,*" whispered that thick voice. "*Morning, morning.*" And the girls heard it loping off toward the castle.

"Daddy!" Bess was sobbing. "I want out of here." But Maddie still held her tightly.

"Wait," she whispered. "Wait till dawn comes, till we know it won't be back."

"What was it?" sobbed her cousin. "It was the Water Horse, wasn't it?"

"Yes," lied Maddie.

She crept to the broken lattice and looked out, but she could barely see a thing. Thick fog wrapped the township. She could see a white glow some distance away and hear the sound of the men's voices. Paul had come back, and someone was dead. Maybe her own parents. Someone else would be dead soon, burned in a roaring fire.

After a few minutes, the cock crowed again, cheerful and heedless. Maddie looked out at the fog. Not so dark as before. The dawn had finally come.

"Bess, run home," she ordered, pushing open the splintered panel, and her cousin disappeared into the fog. But Maddie didn't run home. If her parents were dead, they were dead. Someone else wasn't. Not yet.

She stood hesitating, listening to the shouts of the men, trying to find her way. A torch made a wide red glow in the dimness, coming straight at her. Maddie turned and ran into the formless gray wall of fog toward the invisible castle.

The dark hump of a cottage rose to her right and disappeared into the mist behind her. Beaten-down hillocks of grass appeared at her feet. The thin trunk of a birch tree reeled out of the darkness and almost collided with her.

Clumps of wet grass and uncertain footing. Maddie had reached the bog. She stopped and closed her eyes. I'm taking Lady Mary her breakfast, she told herself, just like I have thousands of times before. My feet know this land, they know the way to the path. She took careful steps, squelching through soft ground, and her feet found the welcome shape of a stepping-stone beneath them.

She opened her eyes. The world was ghostly,

brightening into a foggy autumn morning. The path through the bog lay underfoot. She ran down it, and the bulk of the castle loomed before her, solid in the swirling gray.

Maddie found Paul lying face-up just inside the castle doorway, and the fine belted shirt that her mother had made for him was soaked black with blood. If the men found him like that, they would kill him before he even opened his eyes. How much time did she have? How thoroughly would they search?

Her heart pounding with dread, she unfastened Paul's belt, yanked it from beneath him, and looped it around his ankles. She dragged with all her strength at the free end of the belt, wrapping the leather around her wrists to grip it. As she backed into the darkness of the castle's lowest floor, Paul's insensible body slid after her, his arms flopping help-lessly, and the beltless, bloody shirt rolling up, leav-ing only those English breeches to cover him. On his naked chest, smudged and splashed with blood, Maddie could see the long scars of that other full-moon night.

She dragged him into the far corner, stumbling over planks and shifting trestles and other odd junk out of the way. She worked the bloody shirt over his head and off his arms and then tried to clean away the dark stains, dabbing in the dim light at his wet hands and wiping the stains off his chest. Even his face was splashed with blood, she thought, her breath tight in her throat. Maybe it was her parents' blood. Maybe her mother's.

There's no time for this, Maddie told herself as her eyes stung with tears. Later, after he's safe or dead, then I can cry. She piled the trestles and planks back up, hiding him as well as she could. Then she found the bloody shirt again and stood thinking what to do.

Salt draws out stains. She ran to the salt barrel near the door, scooping out the precious substance with a reckless abandon that would have shocked her mother. She rubbed it into the bloodstains, watching the crystals turn moist and pink as the stains lightened and spread evenly through the cloth. Now to soak it in cold water, she thought, stepping out of the castle doorway.

The fog was already beginning to rise and float away. Maddie's heart almost stopped. Paul's sheepskin blanket lay like a white banner on the dark ground near the path. Had the men looked this way yet? Had anyone seen it? She raced out to grab it and ran back into the darkness, tripping over boards and barking her shin against a block of stone. She pushed aside the junk and laid the sheepskin over the silent carver. He was already burning up with fever.

Maddie grabbed the wadded shirt and hurried out again. She had to soak the shirt and get rid of it, too, before anyone came looking. She ran down the path away from the town until she came to the rotten stump. Then she knelt down on the gravel shore of the loch.

"Cold water for blood," she murmured, plunging the shirt into the icy lake. She rolled a large stone onto it to hold it against the current, smashing her fingers in the process. The loose folds of the trapped shirt billowed underwater like a drowning man struggling for air. Maddie snatched up her own blanket and dried her wet arms. Then she flew up the path through the tatters of mist toward her home and parents.

Fair Sarah was standing by the hearth when Maddie burst in, and she caught her daughter in her arms. "Child, you're like ice!" she exclaimed. "What's this? Blood?" Maddie looked down at the rust-brown smudges across the front of her skirt. She should have been more careful.

James Weaver stood behind Maddie in the doorway, but he didn't come in. His hands were bloody, and the front of his blanket had rust-brown smudges, too. He stared at his wife and daughter without really seeing them, his eyes empty and strange.

"Jamie!" gasped his wife. "Jamie, what's wrong?"

"That was Black Ewan screaming," he muttered. "It caught him between our house and the old barn. He's dead, Sarah. But it's worse than that. It's so much worse than that."

# 15

The men buried Black Ewan beside the stone church while the women keened and mourned. Who now would protect the widows from the specter of hunger? Who would defend the orphans from the enemy's sword? They stood in the dripping weeds as the rain-soaked clouds scudded overhead. Maddie thought, looking around, that the whole world had turned to gray iron.

Normally the men would have watched with the body and made a proper coffin, but they had to bury the farmer in the big dung creel, the great basket that they wheeled about on a barrow. Colin the

Smith, James Weaver, and Horse carried the heavy creel to the muddy edge of the grave.

"That short thing can't be for Black Ewan," muttered Bess in Maddie's ear, "and him such a great big man."

Maddie didn't answer. She knew how such a big man had come to fit into such a short creel. The men had worked for a long time near her house that morning, moving the creel here and there. She had watched them from the doorway as they dropped in one bloody shred after another.

Now the men who carried this grisly burden held it gingerly, as if they wished they could stand farther away from it. They began shoveling mud over it as soon as Father Mac finished the prayers, hiding that terrible secret away beneath the earth.

Black Ewan had died in her place, thought Maddie with an aching heart. He had gone out with his battle-ax to protect his people and found that shadow on its way to her parents' door. He shouldn't have killed Ned, she thought, furious and miserable. With Ned there, the shadow wouldn't have escaped.

"In all the fuss, I can't recall which man I saw

first this morning," reflected Bess unhappily. "I think it might have been Horse. I hope it wasn't. What about you, Maddie? Who did you see first?"

Maddie thought about Paul lying outside the castle, covered with another man's blood. "I can't remember," she lied to her cousin. "I told you it was nonsense."

The funeral over, the men began a cairn where Black Ewan had fallen, bringing large stones to make a mound and swilling the bloodstained earth with water. The women stood by and watched the work, silent and wretched. A bellow rose from the farmer's house, where the cattle still stood patiently in their stalls.

"It's Mad Angus," sighed Janet. "We've forgotten the poor man. Horse, do you go let him out."

The big farmhand reluctantly picked up the key, remembering the blood that had been on it, but Janet's son Lachlan stepped forward and held out his hand.

"I'll do it," he said, and there was no boyish delight in his eyes this time as he took possession of the key. He went into the stable and unlocked the madman from his ring. Then he locked the shackles together.

"Come, old friend," he said gravely to Angus, just as Black Ewan always had done. And after an instant's puzzled hesitation, the giant got up and followed the boy.

Maddie had been afraid that the men would get the dogs and begin hunting the killer, but they huddled by their hearths that afternoon as if they had taken sick. Bess showed everyone the splintered wickerwork on the barn and told the horrifying story of their escape.

"It was the Water Horse," she said. "It almost got Maddie and me. We heard it run away to the loch at the cock crow and splash into the water."

Long after her parents fell asleep, Maddie lay awake. Finally, she dug an ember out of the banked fire and sneaked out into the darkness. The white moon rose in an almost clear sky, and the night was growing bitterly cold. Wrapping her blanket around her, she hurried to the castle.

Paul lay on the bare stone, hot and cold all at once, his teeth chattering and his arms clasped tightly around him. Maddie couldn't take him anywhere warmer. The castle was the safest place. Since Lady Mary's escape and Ned's death, the people avoided the grim building when they could.

But someone might need salt or one of the other odd items stored down in the bottom of the castle and come in and discover Paul by accident. Maddie decided that Lady Mary's floor would be safer. She hoisted Paul up, holding one of his limp arms around her neck, and a sense of self-preservation came alive in the delirious man. He staggered up the stairs, first on his feet and then on his knees, following in some vague way the guidance of her tugs and proddings.

They came up the stone spiral. Echoing darkness and narrow slices of moonlight. Maddie hadn't been in the big hall since the old lady had left it. She retrieved her glowing ember in its little cup and studied the room. A sparse scattering of junk littered the floor, most of it useless, but Maddie seized a fallen tapestry and folded it to make a bed. She half-dragged, half-led the feverish carver to it and laid his blanket over him. But what if he tried to leave? After a short deliberation, she fetched his leather belt and tied his ankles together. That would keep him from walking about in his fever like Mad Angus, and when he came to himself, she hoped it would act as a warning to stay where he was.

Hurrying out into the bitter cold, she went in quest of his shirt. It billowed and shook in the current, its white form eerie in the frosty night. Arms plunged deep into the icy water, Maddie rolled away the rock and retrieved it. I look like the banshee, she thought to herself, like the ghost woman who washes the clothes of the dead, and she imagined how her own relatives would run in horror if they caught the barest sight of her. But her efforts had been rewarded. The shirt was clean. The dark patterns of Black Ewan's blood were gone.

Shivering in the night wind, Maddie hurried back to the castle and laid the shirt out on the floor near the wood-carver. Even under his blanket, the sick young man shook and chattered with the cold, and he gave a low cry at the touch of her chilly hand. Maddie wrapped her own blanket around him and hurried home. She huddled close to her sleeping mother for a long time before she began to get warm.

The next morning, Maddie didn't go to Mass. She stayed inside all day by the fire and spun wool into yarn. She didn't have to wonder anymore where Paul was. He was safe from the weather and from dangerous crowds, and she was looking after him. And she was going to keep looking after him, too, somehow or other.

Late in the night, she set out again with a basket and an ember, creeping among the humps of houses while all good folk slept. It's me they should hang for a witch, she thought grimly as she went her silent way, but her neighbors were finished hunting witches.

Paul was awake, sitting huddled under her blanket beneath Lady Mary's narrow window. "Who's there?" he called in a low voice as she came up the stairs.

Maddie coaxed the little ember out of its bed of ashes. It lit up their faces and the bits of trash that lay about the hall, the belongings of a wealthy woman turned to broken rubbish. Maddie picked up one torn playing card from the floor beside her. The King of Swords. *They'd come at me if they could. The cards know things.*

"Madeleine, what am I doing here?" Paul asked her. "What did I do?" He took the card away in his shaking hand to make her look at him. He had found his clean shirt, she realized, and had belted it on again. There was no sign on it or on him any-more to tell the tale of what had happened.

"They mustn't find you," she warned him. "There's a man dead."

"I killed a man," he gasped. "Who did I kill?"

"Black Ewan is dead," she answered and watched him bury his face in his hands. "It was a judgment on him, Paul," she said. "For what he did to the others."

"I've killed a man," he moaned. "I've never killed a man before."

"It wasn't you that did it, it was God's will," she retorted. "It was God's judgment on him for his wickedness."

But Paul was rocking back and forth, sobbing and running his fingers through his hair, just as Ned's son had before him. Maddie flew at him and grasped his hands, pulling them away.

"It's over and done," she exclaimed, shaking him. "Done, and I'm not sorry. Paul, you've no time to take on, you have to listen to me now. I've brought you some food. Get away from here tonight, go back to fetch your stuff and your tools."

Paul looked up at the mention of his tools and began to pay attention. "I was so far away from here!" he whispered numbly, wiping the tears from his cheeks. "You'd never think I could have walked it in one night."

"Then walk it again," she directed. "Find your things and come back when you have them. It'll be days from now, and you'll not be sick, so no one will ever know."

"Come back!" he cried. "Do you think I can really come back here?"

"You have to," said Maddie. "Ma's so unhappy, she worries so about you, she cries whenever the wind blows." But the young carver just shook his head and buried his face in his hands again.

"I can never come back here," he groaned. "Not after I've killed a man."

"But you will come back!" cried Maddie, and her voice was high and thin. "Just you think what I've done for you, Paul Carver! I've hid you, and I've lied for you, I've walked nights when I should be in bed, I've washed a man's blood out of your shirt just like the banshee woman. I've looked after you like I promised to, and I've saved your life. And you'll come back to me, Paul, you will!"

Paul looked at her. "I'll come back to you, Madeleine," he said.

"Promise!" she demanded fiercely. "You promise me! Swear by your life."

"I swear by my life," he said dully. Maddie thought about that. Ned's son had murdered, too, and he hadn't wanted his life anymore.

"You don't care about your life," she accused. "Promise me by something else, by something you do care about. Swear by your ten bones," and she grasped him by the hands. "Swear by your fingers to come back."

Paul looked down at his fingers. The ten bones that carved, that earned his living. The ten bones that had killed a man. Faint smears of blood still stained his fingers. He knew that they always would.

"I swear by my ten bones," he said, and he held up the hands before her. "I'll come back to you, Madeleine. I promise."

Later, as she lay curled up in the box bed, Maddie thought about Paul. She had saved his life, but hers would never be the same. He was no farmhand like Gillies who could build a house nearby and keep her parents and children fed. He was a vicious killer even if he didn't mean to be, and she knew that he could never stay there. She loved him, and she loved her family, but she couldn't have them both. Maddie sobbed into her blanket in the black of the night and beat her fists against her knees.

The next morning, Maddie decided to check the castle to make sure Paul had left. She passed Little Ian on his way to do some hunting with his dog and his bow.

"I told you true about that Traveler's head," he remarked seriously. "The old man was warning us his time as Churchyard Watcher was up. He didn't tap Black Ewan because of the bad blood between them, but he must have known it would be him, and that's why he was looking so pleased."

Maddie shivered, remembering the sight of that grinning head, and gazed up at the beam of the castle. No head hung there now. Old Ned was gone at last. She hurried up the stairs. Paul had gotten away. She felt the emptiness of his absence and wondered where he might be.

She headed back toward the houses, feeling cold and unwell. Her throat hurt, and her head ached. The late nights and worry were telling on her. As she walked by Paul's favorite boulder, staring dejectedly at her feet, a familiar shadow fell across her path.

"Paul!" cried Maddie happily. She looked up at the boulder, but no one was there. On the ground was the shadow of the carver, turning and shaping something. Above it was nothing at all.

Maddie felt a chill run through her, watching the shadow on the grass. It darkened to an inky blackness and grew in size. It wasn't Paul, and it wasn't holding carving tools, either. Its fingers, turning and flexing, ended in ten long, thin knives.

This time when the girl ran shrieking through town, they bundled her into bed, and the women sat down to keep an eye on her. The townspeople agreed that she was feverish and delirious, just like that carver boy had been. She demanded to see Father Mac, but when he came, she couldn't make any sense.

"Pardon my sins, Father," she begged. "Give me absolution. I helped a shadow to do a murder, and now it's walking around loose!"

"A loose shadow?" inquired the puzzled priest.

"I thought it needed flesh and bones, but it doesn't anymore," she sobbed. "I didn't mean to help it, but I let it get away because he didn't want to do it, it's just his bones that did it, his ten bones with knives at the end. And he'd have died for it, Father, but he shouldn't die; it's not his fault, it's his bones!"

The priest raised his eyebrows at her parents,

and Maddie sensed that he didn't believe her. "Father, it's an evil thing I did," she assured him desperately. "Please pardon me my sins."

"Your fever's talking," the priest consoled her. "You've done nothing wrong."

"But I did, I let the shadow go. I hid it where no one could find it. I didn't want him dead, but I didn't think about the bones all over the town in little pieces, and the graves all dug up. That's why I shouldn't have done it, because of the bones—the bones, and the blood at the castle. But even now, Father, I don't think I could do anything different." She held the priest's big hand. "I just can't do it, I can't see him burn up," she said tearfully. "I'm sorry if it's wrong."

"It's all right," said Father Mac soothingly. "I'm sure we wouldn't want that, either. Try to rest, child. Your mother's worried."

"Absolution," she whispered, clinging to his hand. "Pardon my sins."

The priest considered for a minute. "Is that all you've done?" he rumbled. "You hid a shadow so it wouldn't burn up?"

Maddie closed her eyes. "I lied to Bess in the

barn, and we told fortunes with sieves, and I promised to tell who I saw in the morning, but I didn't."

"At last," sighed the priest gratefully. "Something I understand. All right, young Madeleine, let go of my hand, and I'll give you absolution."

Maddie slept the day away, her head and throat aching. When she woke in the late afternoon, Old Peggy was sitting nearby, humming to herself as she knitted a sock.

"Feeling better?" she wanted to know when she saw that the girl was awake. "Your ma's helping thread the loom. I'll call her if you want."

"I'm not so bad off," Maddie answered. "My throat's a little sore, that's all."

"They said you were raving like Angus."

"I wasn't," sighed the girl. "They just didn't understand."

Old Peggy put down the sock and studied her. "I'm not surprised you have the sight of both worlds," she remarked. "Your grandmother had it, too. She couldn't always tell us what she meant, either. It's a hard gift sometimes."

"Is that what I have, the Second Sight?" wondered Maddie. "I never used to see strange things before."

The old woman shrugged. "Maybe there wasn't much to see. But strange things are happening these days even in our world of flesh. What things are you seeing in the other world?"

Maddie rolled over and propped her head on her hand. "Whenever I go by Black Ewan's cairn, I see fresh blood on the stones," she whispered, "trickles of blood running down the stones and disappearing back into the earth."

"Eh, now, that's not surprising," said Old Peggy, nodding gravely. "Black Ewan's not at peace yet, not with the way he died. His blood still runs where it was spilled because it wants justice done on the killer."

"Why do I have to see it?" demanded Maddie. "I'm not the killer." But, she reflected unhappily, she did know who the killer was.

"I'd say you see it because you're supposed to do something about it," said Old Peggy. "That's the way these things work."

"What am I supposed to do?" asked the girl. "I'm not some big strong warrior like Finn and his Fianna. I can't fight a monster by myself."

"A warrior's strength isn't always the kind that matters," replied Old Peggy. "This is a fight against the shadow world, against the creatures of darkness.

If I were you, I'd pray. It's God Who puts the evil creatures in their place, and it's He Who gave you your gift. Remember this: there's more than one kind of strength. They do say that a little child's laugh is strong enough to vanquish all the demons in hell."

Maddie tried to pray that day and the next, but her prayers weren't the best. Perhaps that was because she couldn't go to church. Her mother kept the ailing girl inside by the fire. Or perhaps that was because her prayers were so angry. They didn't sound much like prayers. Why do I have to have this gift? she asked God. Why did You have to let Paul be bitten? Why couldn't I have fallen in love with Gillies or Thomas? Why didn't Black Ewan leave Ned alone?

As the next few days passed, she felt better and prayed her angry prayers less often. Paul didn't return, and she saw no more strange sights. The town settled back into a routine. Maybe everything was over now, with Black Ewan's death. Maybe Paul was gone for good. He had promised to come back, but he probably hadn't meant it. He had gone off into the wide world, and she would never see him again. As sad as that thought made her, it gave her comfort, too. She knew they could never really be together.

But Paul did come back from the wide world after all. He walked into the town as the first snow fell on the brown thatched houses and began to cover up the frozen mud and golden hills. Maddie looked up from her work, and there he stood in the doorway, with the soft white flakes swirling around him.

Fair Sarah flung her spindle and distaff onto the ground and ran to him with a glad cry.

"Oh, my dear, dear boy!" she exclaimed, hugging him. "It's a blessing just to see you."

# 16

Maddie expected Paul to be uneasy after the murder he'd done, more cautious and bitter than before. Instead, he was relaxed and confident, talking to her parents and playing chess with Father Mac. She, on the other hand, was shy and troubled. It was as if they had changed places.

The first windblown dusting of snow melted, but another soon took its place. This one lingered through a cold, stormy day, and that night it snowed without stopping. The next morning dawned pale and bright, and there was almost no wind. The entire world seemed to have been hushed by the weight of the fallen snow.

"Come with me," said Maddie to Paul, "and I'll show you something."

They wandered out into the silent world. The sky above them was opal and pearl, full of light clouds shadowed with bands of pale blue and purple. The snow reflected the lustrous colors of the sky, and their shadows were a harmless indigo. They crunched along in silence away from the town and the river, following a path that wound into the hills. The path led to a small triangular valley, with a little copse of rowans and birches and a circle of standing stones.

The pair walked among the thin slabs that reared improbably upright. In that gray-and-lavender world, the wet stones were deeply black. Paul reached up and just touched the top of one.

"They're the Nine Maidens," Maddie told him. "Folks say they were girls who went out dancing on Good Friday, and the devil changed them into stone. I never really believed that before, but I don't know, now that I've met you."

Hand in hand, they climbed the nearest snowy hill and sat down to look over the valley, with its spindly, leafless trees and the nine slender black stones in their endless round. The young pair didn't say much. Maddie watched the carver out of the corner of her eye whenever he wasn't watching her. She loved him so. He didn't mean to be a killer. She would keep her promise to Ned.

She pointed at their tracks up the hillside. "We'll have to watch out for that next time," she observed. "If it snows, our trail will give us away."

"There isn't going to be a next time," said Paul.

Maddie's heart filled with dread, and she tightened her grip on his cold hand. He held it tighter in return to steady her.

"It's the only way to fix things," he said. "I need to be gone for good. I'll do something so your ma won't know—fall into the river, maybe. Then Father Mac can still bury me in the churchyard."

"It's a terrible evil to kill yourself," said Maddie. "It can't be the right thing to do."

Paul pulled his hand away, studying the nicks and scars on it from his carving. "But it's not that I want to," he protested. "You know I don't. I have to. The time before last, I woke up and found that you had managed to drive me away from your door. This time I woke up and a man was dead right outside your house. Ned told me a wolf tries hardest to kill the people he loves the best. You say it's justice, that

I came here to kill Black Ewan for Ned. That's not the truth, and you know it. I came back here to kill you."

Maddie stared down at the thin black stones, the slim maidens trapped in their dance. He was right, of course. She couldn't deny it.

"That only happened when you were alone," she countered. "I'll be there next time. You won't get loose again."

"How long do you think I could keep doing this right under your relatives' noses?" he asked. "Do you think they wouldn't find out? That's why a wolf has to wander. You don't know what it means to be among strangers, never having a home. And I don't want you to know what it means. I won't let you go with me."

"Go with someone else, then," she proposed. "Find those other Travelers. They know the secret."

"I don't want to anymore," he said. "It's not worth it to me to live. I've almost killed you twice, and I'm ruining your life. You're getting sick, and you're seeing horrible things. It's the worry eating at you; I know because it eats at me. I'm sorry about Black Ewan. I didn't want to kill him. But, Madeleine, what if it had been you?"

Maddie couldn't think of any more arguments. She didn't know what to say. "It's not right!" she exclaimed. "It isn't right that you have to do this."

"That doesn't matter," he said, trying to console her. "I've had a happy time with you and your family, and I'll have this month, too. I won't ask for any more." Maddie thought of all her angry prayers and felt ashamed of herself.

"I'm glad about it, in a way," he added quietly. "At least now my dying makes sense. You know I wouldn't last long anyway. Sooner or later, we wolves always get found out, just like that girl in the story."

"But you'll tell me?" she pleaded. "Before you go away?" He hesitated. "Please," she whispered, and he gave in.

"All right. I promise I'll say good-bye."

The days passed with dizzying speed, faster than Maddie believed they could. Paul was carving her father a chess set, the pieces beautiful in their stark simplicity. Every day she counted the finished pieces with a sinking heart. Then it was three days before the full moon, and the pieces were all there.

They played a celebratory game over lunch, and Father Mac and the weaver praised the beautiful set again and again. Paul glowed with pride. He teased Fair Sarah and traded stories with the men. He had never seemed so happy

Maddie said nothing. She couldn't even smile. She knew her time was up. Leaving the others over their game, she ran to the little church and threw herself onto her knees in front of the battered wooden statue of the Madonna. She looked at the primitive figures of the Blessed Mother and Child. Paul could have carved a much better one if only he had had time.

"Dear Mother up in heaven, I need help," she begged. "I really, truly need help. I don't want Paul to kill himself, and I don't want my town destroyed, and I don't want my parents and relatives to suffer, with their bones thrown every which way. I love Paul, and I love my parents. I don't want to choose between them. I want them all to be happy together, just like they are right now.

"Please help me, dear Mother of the Shining One. I can't fix this by myself. Ask your Son what I need to do. He knows a way to make it come right; He unties every knot. I promise I'll do whatever God wants if He'll untie this knot for me."

All the rest of the day, Maddie prayed and

prayed, and that night she had a very odd dream. A silvery dawn was breaking. She jumped up from bed and went outside. Not one of the town's inhabitants was nearby in the quiet morning, not even a chicken or sheep. No puff of wind stirred the air. The stillness was profound.

A remarkable stranger stood by Black Ewan's cairn, handsome and tall. He was dressed in a saffron war shirt and fine mail. A cloak of red and blue squares was wrapped around his shoulders, and his boots were the softest leather. His belt was woven of bright colors, and a dagger and a sword hung at his side. On his arms were decorated armbands, and around his neck, a torque collar, but their gold was no brighter than his shoulder-length hair. He held a long javelin, and over his arm hung his round shield, its surface painted with colorful symbols.

Maddie hesitated. Should she fetch the others? No, it would be rude to leave such a noble guest without a word. She stepped forward.

"A blessing upon you," she said shyly.

"And upon you," returned the stranger, still studying the cairn at his feet. "A great battle is coming," he announced.

"We have few to fight in it," Maddie answered,

dismayed. "Is the new lord going to war? Where is the fighting?"

"It will be here," he answered, and he turned to look at her. His eyes were blue, like deep and very clear water, and their force was like a blow. Maddie took a step away and bowed her head, but she could still feel his eyes upon her.

"Don't be afraid," he said.

"I know who you are," she faltered, gathering courage to look up again. "You're one of the Fianna, the hero band who guarded the land in ancient days."

"I am one of the band who guards the land in these days," answered the man. "A great battle is coming to this place. If the young man takes his own life, he will not drive off the spirit within him. He will only leave his corpse behind for that creature to use in its work."

"Paul!" gasped Maddie. "I saw his shadow walking around on its own."

"And so it will walk on its own, with no one to stop it. The people will be hunted one by one until this town becomes a barren place, a place of the dead and the worse-than-dead. You have seen what will happen here, the evil that is coming. You can still escape."

"I don't want to run and leave my loved ones behind," she said. "Isn't there some other way?"

"There is," affirmed the stranger. "Paul can be saved, and so can your town and family, if you truly want that to happen."

"I'll do anything!" she exclaimed eagerly. "Anything you tell me." The stranger looked at her with those eyes like the sea, and Maddie understood. "It's Ned's cure, isn't it?" she whispered, bowing her head. "He was right after all."

"He told you what to do," the warrior agreed. "You are the one who can stop this. Then Paul and your family will be happy, just as they were today."

"I wanted to be happy, too," Maddie said sadly. "I forgot to pray for that, didn't I?"

"God knows what you want," admonished the stranger. "God, Who unties every knot." A faint smile crossed that noble face, as if the words pleased him. "This is a task you must do willingly. This battle is yours to fight."

Maddie looked around at the houses of her town, quiet in that silvery morning. She thought of her relatives who lay inside them. "They won't even know where I've gone," she whispered.

"It is best that they never know," replied the man. "Such creatures as that one would become should not be named aloud."

"But they won't understand," said Maddie, beginning to cry. "My parents won't know why I left them."

The warrior watched her cry for a moment. "Be at peace about this," he said. "In every time, in every land, there are champions of good. Their lives seem small and insignificant, but we remember them, and we rejoice over them. The hosts without number sing their deeds before the Eternal Throne."

Maddie dried her eyes and looked at him in awe. "You are one of the angels of God," she whispered.

"I am the captain of the battle-hosts," he replied. "My name is my war cry. If you fight, you will seem to fight alone, but I will fight with you. I have waited long ages to see this creature brought down to ruin."

Maddie looked again at the silent houses and thought of those she loved, peaceful and happy, with no thought of the terror that was coming. She thought of Paul, giving up his life willingly for her sake. She looked down at Black Ewan's cairn. He had died in this battle, too.

"I will fight," she told him. And then she opened her eyes. She was next to her mother in the box bed, and moonlight poured through the open door. The wind was sighing, and one of the chickens murmured in its sleep.

Maddie climbed out of bed and wandered outside, wide awake and solemn. She went to Black Ewan's cairn. No one stood there in the chilly night, but she didn't feel alone. Beside the rocks grew a small patch of clover, the symbol of the Trinity. She bent and picked a sprig.

"This fight won't last long, Black Ewan," she murmured resignedly to the cairn. "You know that even better than I do. But we have to protect those we love, don't we? That's what you did."

Maddie tucked the clover sprig into a fold of her sleeve and tied it into place with a thread. Warriors went into battle wearing the symbol of their lord. She would do the same.

# 17

That morning, Paul went with Maddie to Mass and watched soberly as she prayed. "Madeleine," he said afterward, "I told your ma and dad that I'm going to sell carvings to the new lord. I won't see you again."

It's time, thought Maddie with a shiver. Time to keep my promise.

"Paul," she said slowly, "I know how you can be cured."

The young carver stared at her in astonishment. "Don't," he demanded, upset.

"No, it's true," she replied. "I learned how from

Ned. There's a creature living with you that makes you change, and I know how to drive it away."

Paul looked around, the mask of caution and worry back on his face. "That can't be true," he stated. "You'd have told me by now, and you'd be happier about it. There's no cure for what I am."

"I couldn't tell you before," she said in a low voice. "It's—it's hard to do, that's all. But not hard for you. All you do is change one more time."

"What do you do that's hard?" he asked. "I want to know about it."

"I can't tell you," said Maddie. "It has to be a secret."

The young man had been calm and composed, ready to die. Now all his plans were for nothing. "I don't want to change again," he protested angrily. "I want to be done with this."

"You will be," she promised. "You'll be cured, you really will. Just one more time, Paul. Please."

He frowned at her, unhappy and uneasy. "All right," he muttered. "But this is the last time. And it's not how I want it."

Maddie gave him a little smile. "You'll see," she said. "It's better than your way. I'll meet you tomorrow by the rotten stump." She watched as he walked out of town.

Kneeling on the stone step of the confessional next morning, Maddie tried to collect her thoughts. Be prepared for death, Father Mac had told her, and she had intended to. She wanted to make a really good confession of her sins so that her mind could be at peace as she died, but her mind was wandering dreadfully, and she couldn't remember what she had planned to say. There had been the time when her mother had been tired and she hadn't carried the baskets for her. How she regretted that now! And the time when her father had been discouraged and she hadn't bothered to smile at him. If only she could go back and do it! If only it weren't too late.

Maddie ranged sadly over these odd little omissions and faults of long ago, and on the other side of the curtain, Father Mac's astonishment grew. He had never heard such a confession from her before. At length she ran out of regretful memories, and he gave her absolution. She rose, about to go say her penance, but then she turned back to the priest. Second Sight or no Second Sight, she shouldn't trust a dream. It would be better to make sure.

"Father, I was wondering," she said slowly. "If a fellow went and got himself killed—not that he died by his own hand, mind, and not that he wanted to die, but to save the life of other people—that wouldn't be suicide, would it?"

"No, it wouldn't," came the cautious answer. "A suicide dies because he doesn't want his life anymore. But if that person truly wanted to live and would live if he only could, then his death would be like a warrior's death, a sacrifice for others."

"Good," she said. "This person is like that." She started to turn away, but the priest blocked her path, his face a study of puzzlement and concern.

"I'm worried about you lately, young Madeleine," he declared. "I'm worried about you now. What do you say about that?"

"I'm sorry if you're worried," Maddie replied politely. "It's my ma who'll be worried next if I'm not back home soon." And she left the priest to his thoughts.

But Maddie couldn't bear to spend her last day with her mother. Instead, she visited Bess and helped her tired aunt with the children. Will they miss me? she wondered sadly. Probably the little ones won't even remember their cousin Maddie.

"Bess, I have to go somewhere," she said as they milked the sheep. "But don't tell anyone. Just say I went home."

Bess had tried in vain to awaken her cousin's high spirits. She looked at her now with a thoughtful frown.

"And when will you be coming back?" she demanded.

"I don't know," Maddie answered. "Don't bother looking for me this evening."

"I know what you're doing," announced Bess with confidence. "You're running away with that carver boy."

"I am not!" gasped Maddie, caught completely off-guard. "Bess, how could you say such a thing!"

"Oh, yes, you are, and I don't blame you a bit," replied her cousin cheerfully. "I'd run off with him, too, he's that good-looking."

Upset and irritated, Maddie hurried through the gloomy afternoon. Paul met her at the rotten stump, and they raced down the path to beat the moonrise. There was no time and no breath for talking.

Inside the cave, Paul retrieved his lighted lantern and led the way to the chain and collar. He buckled it around his neck as she sat down to catch her breath.

"I know what you're going to do," he announced.

Maddie stared at him in the speckled light from the pierced lantern sides. "You do?" she exclaimed in amazement.

"You're going to wait until I'm changed, and then you're going to call the men to kill me," he said. "That way I don't have to kill myself. I'm glad. I didn't mind doing it, but they say suicides never find peace for their souls. I'd like a little peace now, I think."

Maddie moved the lantern so that the open side faced him and the candlelight shone out onto him. He was so handsome and courageous, facing death to keep her safe. For the first time, she thought about how he would feel when he woke up and found her dead.

"Paul, I'm doing the right thing," she told him. Tears came to her eyes. "I know things, Second Sight things. This is the only way. It's like Father Mac says, this life's just a test. We have to look beyond the grave."

"I know," he said, and he smiled at her. A lump rose in her throat.

"You—you have to not mind," she insisted as the tears ran down her cheeks.

"I don't mind. Don't cry," he said. "Good-bye, Madeleine."

"Good-bye, Paul," she whispered. She turned away so she wouldn't see him change. After a minute, she heard the chain begin to rattle as he paced.

"Come here," he demanded sharply. "Come *here!*" And she knew that Paul was gone.

Maddie took off her blanket, folding its length carefully. There was no need for it to be ruined. Then there was the problem of the lantern. She wanted to blow it out so she wouldn't see anything, but Paul would need it later, after the cure. She closed the little shutter as far as she could and turned its bright face to the wall.

"Come *here! Come here!*" Now the voice was rough and thick. She heard the metal clashing of those terrible knifelike claws.

"I'm coming," she replied, turning to face it.

Dimming the light hadn't done her much good. She couldn't see its outline in the blackness of the cave, but those huge green eyes with their tiny dots of pupils gleamed down at her. It hissed and bubbled, and the great eyes blinked. *"Liar!"* it spat.

216

Maddie's stomach flopped and tingled as if it were full of frogs. "I'm not lying," she asserted as boldly as she could. "I'm going to let you kill me."

The creature stirred and paced in the shadows, clashing its claws. Those round green eyes never left her face.

"They *all* let me kill them," it sneered in a bubbling purr. "They always run so *slowly*."

Maddie felt the cave start to spin, and she staggered back a step. She closed her eyes and remembered why she was there.

"Nasty *worm*," it slavered. "*Worse* than a worm! Worms are soft and sweet, but you're full of crunchy hard *knobs*."

"Shut your face!" she screeched. "Or I won't do it." She knelt down and pressed her shaking hands together to pray. No words came, but a little glow of courage warmed her heart. She felt for the sprig of clover. She tried to stand up again, but her legs were like blocks. Maybe she could just crawl.

"You *won't* do it," snarled the creature. "You'd never *dare* to do it. Three steps, that's all, just *three steps*. I'm so *hungry*!" Its voice rose into a whine. "But *you* won't do it!" It flung itself angrily to and fro. "Smelly little *liar*!"

She had lied, Maddie realized, shivering all over. She couldn't possibly go up to it. She thought of Paul's corpse stalking the town, of the bones of her parents and neighbors. I will fight with you, the angel had said. She looked for another way.

"If you'll stay at the end of your chain," she faltered, "I'll come to that corner by you. I—I promise I will. But you have to look away. Look away—and count to fifty." She wasn't thinking very well. "Or do you—can you count?"

"I could count the stars in the *sky*," it boasted. "I could count the sand in the *desert*. I've counted every spurt of blood through your heart since the day that you were born. *Waiting. Waiting* for my *chance*."

The dark cave was spinning and spinning. Maddie put her hand on the rough wall. "Count fifty more," she gasped, "and you'll have your chance." Still those eyes shone down unmoving. Maddie roused herself with an effort. "I thought you were hungry," she whispered.

The huge form shuffled sideways down the length of the chain, and the green eyes vanished.

Remember Paul, Maddie told herself, licking her lips. Remember Ma and Dad. Crawl forward. Crawl to the chain. Then it will all be over. She squeezed her eyes tightly shut and crawled along, her shoulder brushing the wall. Time passed, and she came to the bend of the cave. The wall curved before her into a rough corner, and she curled up into it. She was panting for breath, and sweat was dripping onto her hands and into her eyes. She heard the links rattling above her, and a scraping, grating noise.

"*You can't get away,*" announced that thick voice. "*Now you're going to die.*" Maddie didn't answer. Her mouth was as dry as dirt.

"I've never seen *anything* like it," it bubbled. "You can't *wait* to be *eaten*." It laughed, hideous and slavering. "You must be *mad*."

Curled up tight, she felt it coming nearer, felt the cold chain coil across her body. "You little *fool*," it gloated in her ear, so close that she felt numb from the icy chill it gave off. "You're *mad*, that's what you are! You're *mad*! You're—MADELEINE!"

A scream tore from the monster, right over her head. One scream after another, long, high wails of evil and anguish. Far away in the night, the townspeople heard those screams and froze in terror. In the closeness of that black cave, they were heart-stopping.

The chain sang, snapping taut and loosening as

the creature writhed in the darkness. The air was full of the clashing of its claws and the scrabbling of its huge body. Still it screamed and snarled and cursed, now to one side of her and now to the other. Stones crashed and slammed into the walls and ceiling. Their battering report echoed down the passages.

Maddie, pressed as tightly as she could be into the corner, sank closer to the ground. She was only dimly aware of the thrashing form. The one thing approaching a thought in her mind was a feeling of hurt disapproval. She had hoped that it would all be over by now.

Slowly the screams died down into long wails and then into moans. The clashing quieted, the churning ceased, and the moans became sobs. The chain loosened above her once more as the figure crawled forward and flung a sweat-drenched hand across her huddled body.

But Maddie didn't feel it. She didn't feel anything. Her mind had escaped the gloom of the cave into a deeper darkness.

## 18

Maddie opened her eyes to find her mother looking down at her.

"I had such a dream, Ma," she said. Then she glanced around in surprise. She was at home in bed. She sat up, shaky and queasy. The settle by the door was empty. "Where's Paul?" she wondered.

"You're awake to stay this time?" her mother wanted to know, and Maddie could see that she'd been crying. "Jamie, she's awake," she called, and Maddie's father came over. He knelt down by the bed, and Fair Sarah sat down on a stool, and they both looked at her, their faces grave.

"Where's Paul?" she asked them again.

"Maddie, tell us what this is all about," said James Weaver seriously.

"What do you mean?" she asked. "What what's about? Where's Paul?"

"Father Mac came here last evening," replied her father, "and when he saw you weren't home, he was very concerned. We went to Colin the Smith's house, but you weren't there either, and Bess said you had run away with Paul. It was black night by then, and we could hear that creature on the loose. I was afraid we'd never find you alive. God knows how he knew, but Father Mac had an idea you'd be at the Cave of the Arrows, and we found you and Paul there together."

"Black night, and you found Paul? Really Paul?" asked Maddie slowly. She looked at their troubled faces, and her heart stopped in her breast. "He's dead!" she shrieked. "Paul's dead! Oh, no!" She burst into loud tears.

"Maddie, saints above!" cried James Weaver, startled. "What sort of dad do you think I am? Of course I didn't kill the boy." He patted her heaving shoulders awkwardly. "There, there, calm down.

Paul isn't dead. I just want you to tell me what you were doing, that's all."

"But he isn't dead, truly?" sobbed Maddie, unable to sort this through. "It was full night, and full moon, and he was Paul, and not dead?" She paused, bewildered. "And I'm not dead, either?"

"Maddie, no one's dead," replied her father patiently. "No one that we know of, anyway. Paul met us in the cave passage, struggling along with you, and I'm bound to say he was just as senseless as you are. He kept crying out to look for a bite, were you bitten—spider, snake, or dog, we never could find out. Then we got outside the cave and he just stood and stared at the moon, and not another useful word did we hear all the way home. He couldn't be trusted not to walk right into the water. Father Mac had to lead him by the hand. Your mother searched for that bite, but she didn't find anything, only that you'd fallen into a faint."

"So Paul's not dead." Maddie sobbed more quietly, calming down. "And I'm not dead, either," she remarked with some surprise. She looked at their worried faces again. "Then what's the matter?" she asked.

"What's the matter? You ran off!" exclaimed her father, exasperated beyond all patience. "Maddie, how on earth could you do such a thing and then ask us what's the matter?"

Good sense began to return. Maddie considered this statement carefully. All in all, she could see their point.

"But we didn't run off," she protested. "That was Bess's own notion, and I told her before I left what I thought of it."

"Then what did you do?" asked the weaver.

"Didn't Paul tell you?" asked Maddie. Her father shook his head.

"Only that he never meant to harm you," he said. "That he'd have died before he'd have let it happen, whatever that means. Maybe he's telling Father Mac. They're together in his cottage. Let what happen? That's what I want to know."

Maddie took a deep breath and thought things over. The last three months had given her lots of practice in lying, but she didn't want to lie. On the other hand, looking at their worried faces, she didn't want to tell them the truth.

"Paul and I went hunting for that thing that killed Black Ewan," she told them. "I'd been to the cave, and so had Father Mac, because that's where I found Paul when he collapsed with the fever. I remembered seeing something strange there." She paused for breath, and inspiration struck. "The cave opening had been widened by something, as if a big animal was inside. There were chunks of rock lying all around. After Black Ewan got killed, I fell to thinking about it, and I told Paul I meant to go inside. He thought I was being silly, but he agreed to go along.

"We did see something in the cave—a shape or a shadow, I don't know. We heard it screaming right by us. I thought we were both of us dead, and I fainted. Paul must have thought the same."

James Weaver and Fair Sarah glanced at each other, puzzled and questioning. It sounded very unlikely, but, then again, nothing else seemed any more likely.

"Maddie, this is the stupidest thing you've ever done," said her father. "We heard the thing screaming, too, but far away, and it never came any closer. I'll go with the men as soon as it's daylight to find out what's in that cave. The whole town will be buzzing over Bess's story about how you two meant to run off, but Paul's a good lad, and I'll stand by him. He has more brains than the other boys here, this night's work aside."

"I knew it was just nonsense," said Fair Sarah, her voice shaking. "I knew I should have slapped Bess as soon as I heard it. You wouldn't ever leave us, child, and my boy knows he has no call to run off. Where would he go, I'd like to know," she demanded angrily, "and him with not a soul left in the world? And like as not still feverish, too, and who would make him his herb drink then?"

Maddie took a long look at her mother's tear-stained face. "You don't want Paul to leave us," she declared triumphantly. "You want him to stay at our own hearthside so you can look after him."

James Weaver smiled at his wife's determined expression. "She has her heart set on it," he admitted.

Maddie slept later than she ever had, blissfully free from worry. When she opened her eyes, her parents were gone. James Weaver was with the men deep in the cave, marveling at the iron chain and stout collar, at the deep gouges carved into the rock floor and the chunks of stone hurled about. Fair Sarah was at the blacksmith's house telling Bess and her mother

Maddie's tale before Bess had time to tell the town her own.

Only Paul was in the house, sitting on the settle near the doorway and cleaning the mud from his boots before he put them on. Maddie stared at him curiously. He didn't look the same as before. His cheeks had color in them now, and so did his hands. He looked up and smiled at her, and her heart skipped a beat. "Good morning," he said.

Maddie felt shy. She didn't know whether to burst with pride and happiness or die of embarrassment. She got up and wandered over to the hearth to warm her hands.

"You have to tell me what you did in the cave," Paul said. "To cure me. What did you do?" He looked at her, but she wouldn't look at him now. "Please tell me, Madeleine," he insisted. "I need to know."

"I had to wait until you were changed and then let you tear me apart," she said. He sat there, stunned, and she decided she would die of embarrassment after all. "It was the only way," she went on quickly. "It's the only cure for werewolves. Ned told me about it, and I prayed for a way you and my parents could both be happy. That was the answer to my prayer."

"The answer to a prayer?! How could you pray for such a thing? As if I could be happy after I killed you!"

"But I wanted you to be happy," she pointed out.

"And I wanted you to be alive," he answered. "Why do you think I was going to kill myself? I don't want you dead, Madeleine, not ever."

Maddie laughed. "I'll die someday," she reminded him cheerfully. "I'm thinking it won't be so bad."

"You sound like Father Mac," he said. "He had me in at his cottage all night last night, talking about things like that. I told him what happened, and he says he won't tell. I think I can trust him. He's sure no one ever baptized me, so he's going to do it once I've learned enough." Maddie giggled at the thought of a grown man being baptized, and Paul grinned sheepishly. "He says I'll be his newest parish baby.

"He told me he has news of Lady Mary, by the way. She's the housekeeper for a priest who's an old friend of his. He says her cooking is terrible, but they have splendid arguments. She goes to Mass just so she can criticize his sermons."

Maddie warmed her hands and smiled over the news, at peace with the whole world. "My parents were raving," she remarked, looking down at the burning peat.

"I'll say," Paul answered, tugging on a boot. "Your ma cried and kissed me and threatened to beat me with her broom. But your dad thinks my carving will be a help to the town, and, anyway, carving isn't all I know to do. I've worked harvests and herding and slaughtering, and I can turn my hand to lots of things. I kept Ned supplied with drink for years. I'm thinking my family won't starve."

My family. That was Maddie and her parents. Feeling happy, she sat down beside him to watch him lace his boot.

"If you want to come with me, you'd better escape now," he observed. "Your ma will be back soon. She's bound to keep you wrapped in blankets all day and feed you some awful brew."

Maddie got up to fetch her blanket. "Where are we going?" she wanted to know.

"We're hunting for wood," he told her. "A special piece of wood. I don't think Father Mac can have his new Madonna by Christmas, but with a little luck, he'll have it by Easter."

## acknowledgments

Sincere thanks to my editor, Reka Simonsen, for caring just as much as I do about our books at every stage of their development and progress.

Heartfelt thanks to Ross Noble, member of the Historic Environment Advisory Council for Scotland and curator emeritus of the Highland Folk Museum, for his many constructive suggestions and his invaluable assistance in correcting the manuscript for historical accuracy.

Special thanks to Father Nicholas Mary, C.Ss.R., of Golgotha Monastery in the Orkney Islands, for his assistance in researching the historical and religious background of this story and for his prudent, perceptive criticisms of the manuscript.